PHENEX

Fire From Heaven - Book 3

AVA MARTELL

GET IN TOUCH

Sign up for Ava Martell's newsletter to receive updates on new releases as well as free sneak previews of what's coming next in the Fire From Heaven series.

Follow Ava on social media

Facebook
Twitter
Tumblr
Instagram

Official site
avamartell.com

Author's note:

*If you're new to the series,
it's recommended to read
in the following order:*

*1. Lucifer
2. Archangel
3. Phenex
4. Grace
5. Gabriel - coming spring 2020
6. Raphael - coming winter 2020
7. Apocrypha - coming spring 2021*

For those lost in the darkness

PHENEX

C old.
   Black.
   Alone.

Darkness so deep, so unending that I can't keep myself from running my fingertips across my face, reassuring my tattered mind that I still have eyes, that they haven't been plucked from my skull leaving behind empty sockets to gaze blindly at nothing.

I shiver, and the full-bodied shudder wracks my frame. I pick at my memories, trying to recall the last time I was warm and coming up empty. The half-remembered sensation of sunlight on my face bleeds away to scraps of nothingness.

There's only the cold and the darkness of the void surrounding me. Dulled by my blindness, my other senses scrabble to compensate, but they discover little. The dampness of the rough stone floor beneath me seeps through my suit, the light linen feeling as thin as paper. I squint at where I know my arm is, my pupils searching for the tiniest shaft of light to illuminate the cream colored fabric.

Nothing.

I shift, rocking back and forth, the movement almost unconscious at this point. The thick iron links of the chain around my neck clatter against the floor, the hollow noise impossibly loud in the silence. The chain puddles beside me, a dozen yards of enspelled iron making me as weak as a human. Weeks or months or years ago, I crawled to the end of the tether and never once found a wall. Somehow the exposure makes it so much worse.

I wrap my arms around myself, resting my forehead on my knees as the panic rises. It's been too long. She'll be coming soon, and I don't know how much more of this I can bear.

In the first days inside my prison, I wished for a rack. Wished for torture. I could contend with blood and pain, but not the perpetual darkness and silence and solitude. I'm sure she knows this.

Time slips away into nothing. Days, weeks, months. Perhaps years. Maybe the sun has finally swallowed up the Earth and this place is all that's left. Bit by bit, I feel fragments of myself break off and crumble away.

I thought many things in those first days, and the part of me that still remembers wants to laugh at how I wished for torture. How I thought anything was better than unending nothing.

The silence breaks with the *click click click* of heels on the damp stone. The steps circle me, slow and measured. There is no fear in those footsteps, no hesitation. I am at her mercy, and she knows it. She *likes* it.

The footsteps stop, and I turn my head toward where I think she stands, squinting sightless eyes into the empty air. An instant later a slender hand grabs my jaw, long nails digging into my skin as she tilts my head upward, forcing me to look up at her.

I still see nothing, but I know somewhere in the darkness she's smiling.

"Soon." The whisper slides across my senses like a caress. I've long since lost count of the days since I came here, and another voice, even that of my jailer, is a balm to my starved senses.

I'm not quite broken yet.

I lash out at her, springing to my feet, my fingers ready to claw at her face and tear through those eyes until she's trapped in the same darkness I am.

My hands close around empty air.

"That was a mistake."

Her voice is calm. She expected the attack, but that doesn't mean she will let it go unpunished.

Her footsteps recede as she walks away, and I listen in the silence for the sound of a door.

Then the pain begins, and I hear only my own screams.

I CALL FOR HIM.

I know where I am. I always knew.

I am an angel, after all, not some weak mortal soul clinging to denial. I've spent too many years in Hell to not recognize it.

In the beginning, I rail against my captivity, ripping at the rough metal of the chain until my fingers are sticky with blood. I pull at the tether like a shackled dog, the iron collar cutting into my neck, choking the breath from my throat. I scream curses to the walls, threats and promises of what will become of my captors when I free myself.

Of course, I will free myself.

But days slip into weeks with no way to count time save my own heartbeat, and the first tendrils of self-doubt crawl into my mind like a parasite, sapping the fight from me.

And I call for him.

This is *his* kingdom. His world.

"*Lucifer!*"

I scream his name until my voice fails, my ravaged vocal cords giving out as the echoes die in my ears and the threads of guilt and fear tighten around my heart whispering *worthless* and *unwanted* and *fallen* like a twisted mantra.

Why doesn't he come?

He said I was forgiven. Lucifer barred me from returning to Hell out of kindness, not vengeance. He knew my hatred for every cell of this place because he shared it. I followed him, fighting my brothers and sisters because his words of freedom and free will and choice made sense to me. And when Michael banished him here, I followed because no one else would. Not for the right reasons.

Lucifer was many things after the Fall. He could be the cruel taskmaster when it was needed to quell the infighting as the other Fallen vied for his favor. He could be vicious to the souls that deserved it, but I know he hasn't forgotten those first days, dragging his shattered wings through the barren fields of the damned. Whatever I did, Lucifer wouldn't abandon me here.

Then why doesn't he come?

My cries grow fainter and fainter as my resolve falters, and the weak murmurs of "Lucifer" barely reach my own ears.

Why doesn't he come?

Millennia upon millennia of memories stack together like bricks, years of camaraderie in the trenches, of shared hatreds and unspoken regrets, of blood and temptation.

I made a mistake. He of all people should understand the cruelty of being condemned for one wrong choice.

But then why doesn't he come?

She does. She doesn't speak to me again. She could silence her steps, but she always allows me to hear them. *Click click click* on the stone. *Click click click* as pain creeps closer.

She never touches me again, never draws close enough to let her scent reach my nose, though the faint waft of lush flowers clung to my skin for days after her first visit. Whatever she is, she's powerful, creating the tools of her trade out of raw magic and her own will.

A whip cuts silently through the air, the first lash hard enough to leave me sprawled on my stomach as she flays open my back. I bite my tongue until I taste copper as I fight to stay silent as each lash rains down.

I hear a chuckle in the darkness at that. My resistance amuses her.

Another day brings fire – flames without light, without heat. I'm still cold and blind, trapped in darkness thick as tar, and it takes too many minutes before I register that the agony I'm feeling is my own flesh blistering and charring.

She watches in silence. I stop holding in the screams that day.

Every time, the pain continues until my mind gives out and my weakened body plunges into blissful unconsciousness only to awaken later whole and unmarred.

Sometimes she does nothing. *Click click click.* She pauses a few feet away and stands in silence, watching as I shrink further into myself, every muscle tightening in anticipation of today's agony. My breath comes short as I wait, dizziness clouding my mind as I fight the useless urge to run, to hide, to beg.

I almost want the torture to begin, if only because then it can end.

And she knows it. She stays until I can't hide the tremors anymore, until what my own mind has conjured is enough to rip me in two, and I'm left whimpering like a child in the darkness. Then she leaves me to my own terror and the *click click click* fades into silence.

Those days are the worst.

And then one day, I break.

The pain begins, another blur of blood and anguish that will go on and on. The idea of escape has long since disintegrated. There is nothing left of me, and I slip away into some forgotten corner of my mind. There I stay, safe and hidden, the torment outside unable to reach me.

This angers her. She wanted to break me, but once her toy is well and truly shattered it's not nearly as amusing. She curses me, tightening the collar until my breath cuts off, and drags me to my feet.

I obey, as limp and docile as a rag doll, facing the scene with blank detachment. Some spark within me wonders if I would recognize my own face anymore. She shakes me, trying to rip some reaction out of me, but I disappear deeper into myself. She lets me go, and I slump to the floor like a marionette with its strings cut, and I know no more.

Time passes. It might be hours or months. It might even be years that I spend slumped on the cold stones, burrowing deeper and deeper into myself until light rouses me.

The *click click click* is coming closer, and I want to shrink away, to crawl back into the safe hideaway I created, but with every step, the light grows brighter. The conjured glow is dim, barely enough to illuminate a foot in front of her, but after so long in darkness, I squint at the glare.

She's dragging someone behind her, a cowed creature in a stained and bloody dress, and some part of me flares to life as I recognize another angel. The same chains that bind me coil around her, and our jailer wastes no time in bolting her to the floor.

The dazed angel jolts at the sound of the chain striking the floor, her lips curling back from her teeth as she tries to launch herself at our tormentor. Unconcerned, she clutches her hand into a fist and the angel freezes, clawing at the collar as it tightens around her neck.

For the first time, I look at the face of my nightmare. She's beautiful, dark eyes above sharp cheekbones, dark hair swept up to bare a slender neck. She's the sort that in another life I would have shared a few hours or a few days with, ticking off my favorite sins. She's lovely, and those dark eyes hold nothing but contempt.

She'll torture us both until there's nothing left, and she'll sleep just fine tonight.

She drops the glowing orb at her feet and stalks away without a word. The dim light flickers at the impact but continues to glow. I wonder how long until it burns out and we're left in darkness again.

I hear the scrape of metal against stone, and I turn to see my new companion pulling ineffectually against the chains.

"Don't bother," I say, my voice cracking with disuse. "I already tried."

Defeated, she drops the chain. Her back is to me, but I still see her thin shoulders quaking as she fights to hold back the sobs. She takes a deep breath, steadying herself before turning to face me.

"I'm Caila," she whispers.

"Phenex."

She tenses at my name. I only vaguely recognize her, though I'm sure our paths crossed before the Fall. But every good little angel knows of Lucifer's right hand.

The pretty one who trails behind Lucifer like a pet, begging for his scraps while dreaming of Heaven. We laugh at you.

Uriel's words echo in my head, but the blonde angel shakes off her hesitation and moves closer to me.

"How long have you been here?"

I shrug, sinking down to the floor. The fog surrounding my brain has cleared for the moment, but I don't know how long it will last. I don't know how long I *want* it to last.

I look at Caila, taking in the tendrils of pale hair framing her face. Rusty streaks of dirt and dried blood stand out on her pale skin, and her wide eyes track my every movement.

She doesn't trust me, and I almost have to laugh at that.

"You know where we are, don't you?" I ask. My voice sounds as if I haven't spoken for years, and I suppose that's accurate. My curses and cries of Lucifer's name faded into inarticulate screams and animal moans long ago. I'm almost shocked my tongue remembers how to form speech.

Caila shakes her head, the tangled flax of her hair shifting with her movement.

Like a halo, my mind supplies, and I fight back a giggle at the thought.

"Hell," I state flatly. "You're in Hell."

Something in her cracks at the confirmation of what she no doubt suspected. Her eyes widen, the whites almost too bright to look at, and she springs to her feet, twisting her fingers through the links of the chain and pulling with all her might.

I watch her struggle impassively, the memory of my own futile battle with the chain still too fresh. She pulls, the iron cutting into her fingers, ripping the delicately lacquered fingernails and rubbing her palms raw. The chains do not break. The bolt in the floor doesn't even have the decency to creak.

Hell was not made for hope.

Abruptly the fight drains out of her. Her shoulders slump and the chain falls from her bleeding fingers, the sound of the links crashing to the floor ringing in the silence.

She stands still, the flickering light of the orb deepening the shadows under her eyes, and even millennia upon millennia in Hell makes it impossible to do anything but pity this creature.

When she finally speaks again, her voice is barely above a

whisper, but it's as clear as a shout. "What does she want with us?"

I think of the hatred in her dark eyes, of year upon year of silent torment, of the *click click click* as pain draws nearer, and I stare at Caila's stricken face for a moment before replying.

"I don't know."

The one thing that's certain is our captor didn't put us together out of the kindness of her heart. This sweet-faced angel with her sad eyes and pretty dress won't last long, and something tells me that when she breaks it'll be the end of us both.

THE LIGHT WITHERS SLOWLY, the darkness creeping incrementally closer. It's such a subtle progression that I doubt Caila even notices it, but my light-starved eyes do. Blindness is crawling towards us both like a slithering insect, and I can't help thinking our jailer's skills are wasted on Earth. She managed to succeed where even Hell's cruelest torturers could not.

How many humans could splinter an angel with a glorified light bulb?

The light has faded to almost nothing when Caila breaks out of her terrified stupor long enough to comprehend it.

"What happens when it goes out?"

I don't answer for the longest time. We're both at the very end of our tethers, huddled a few scant feet from the dying light like ancient humans crouching by a fire to fend off the circling wolves.

I don't have the heart to tell her that this is the first light I've seen since I came here.

I don't have the heart to tell her I expect this will be the last.

Has it been days since Caila was thrown into the cell with me? Weeks? Caila's apprehension at being locked up with a fallen angel dropped away quickly. Whatever my past crimes might be, they are no more substantial than dust in our current situation.

She leans her small frame against mine, her head tucked under my chin. Her hair tickles my nose when she shifts restlessly, her eyes never leaving the faint radiance of the orb.

"Heaven has changed."

She lets the statement hang in the air, and I wait as she gathers her words. The orb flickers, going dark for an instant before the glow steadies.

"I'm beginning to think that Lucifer was right." She doesn't move, doesn't turn to face me, and I'm not surprised that this place gives her the courage to lend voice to her darkest thoughts. Hell was made for confessing your sins.

"The archangels. . . they're not what they were." Somehow in the shadows, my hand finds hers. I feel the ragged edges of her fingernails and the lingering stiffness of dried blood on her skin. Her fingers rest slack for a moment before gripping mine back.

Any port in the storm.

She leans forward, twisting her head to look at me, and I miss the contact already and it terrifies me. Just as I know the coming darkness will be even more terrible after this brief respite, I know the solitude will destroy me once Caila is taken from me.

I have no doubt she will be taken from me.

"I admired Uriel once," she murmurs, her eyes falling to our entwined hands. "I believed in him. The archangels were supposed to be the best of us. Our leaders in Father's absence." Her voice falters, and her head lifts, her eyes gazing out into the darkness. "He turned into a killer, a madman tearing down innocent lives for what he thought was right. We're supposed to protect them!"

The orb flickers again, and the darkness lingers just a bit longer before the light returns.

"We were supposed to protect them," Caila repeats, the energy draining out of her. The darkness and the silence has a way of stripping away our illusions, tearing away all those comforting lies we tell ourselves to endure each day. In here, there's nothing to hide behind, and the truth comes roaring in like a flash flood, and once that current takes you, there's no fighting it.

"They don't need our protection." Caila tenses at my words, but doesn't comment. "They need us to stop meddling in their lives, but it's not surprising Father's first forgotten children are curious about their replacements."

She shakes her head ever so slightly, a silent denial of what she knows to be truth. Her scent surrounds me, so different than the twin scents of damp stone and old blood around us. Caila smells of sunlight, honeyed pollen and hothouse blooms, the same golden, thick scent that rode the air of the Garden. Innumerable centuries have passed since I set foot inside that sanctuary but I'll never forget what it smelled like inside the gates. Even Uriel's perpetual glowering couldn't keep me away back then.

Underneath the flowers and warmth and *life* is the same hint of ozone all angels have – the scent where the atmosphere grows thin and snow is born, the sharpness on the wind as a storm rolls in. The reminder that even the most deceptively delicate of us still holds the power of a hurricane in our wings.

She smells like home, and for the first moment since I came here I wish Uriel had killed me. If I'd bled out on the floor of The Saint, there would be nothingness.

There would be peace.

The orb sputters, the spark illuminating it blinking on and off in rapid succession before finally failing, plunging us both into darkness. For a few moments longer, I see the ghost of the orb, as though I'd stared at the sun long enough to scorch my retinas, but that fades too.

"Phenex?" The blackness around us seems to swallow up Caila's voice, making her sound miles away even though she's pressed against my chest. My fingers tighten around hers as the darkness presses in, silently telling her, *I'm here* and *hold on* and *have hope* because I know she'd hear the lie in my voice.

The light is gone. We're still together, but I strain my ears for the familiar *click click click* that signals our nightmare is starting again.

2

CAILA

Hell was quiet.

I never expected that – the suffocation of silence trapping you inside your own head, the complete lack of outside stimulation forcing you to revisit every mistake and every sin that led you to your current predicament. You feel wrapped in cotton wool as memories of *color* and *light* and *hope* are dulled with each minute that ticks away, but some primal sliver of your brain remains laser focused on where the inevitable next torment will issue from.

Hell is a world with all the noises dampened until the only sound is your own heartbeat and the slow swish of blood pumping through your veins as you wait.

Even the grave has noise, the creeping scratches of insects and the plod of decay as roots and worms do their work. The Earth is never silent, and the bodies rotting in the soil have more voices than the inhabitants of the cold cells of Hell.

Once the light flickered out, even a whisper felt too loud, but we forced ourselves to speak, murmuring long rambling stories of our travels across Earth, of the civilizations we watched rise from nothing and others that crumbled to ash. Our voices dropped even lower when we spoke of those outside that we cared for, as though speaking their names in the darkness would curse them to suffer beside us. Those hushed voices tore through the silence, a reminder that a world still existed outside of our tomb.

I don't know how Phenex survived alone in that place for as long as he did.

New Orleans is what passes for quiet now. It's half past four in the morning, and I'm alone on the cracked cement stairs, gazing out into the scraggly grass of the backyard lit by the weak light of a single unbroken streetlamp.

The faint sound of cars on the freeway rumbles like a distant storm. The black sky at the edge of the horizon has just started the slow fade into purple that will slide into the dazzling light of morning in a few short hours. I gulp down the humid air, forcing myself to tamp down the panic that rises in my throat like bile whenever I think of that place.

I'm alive. I'm free.

It's over.

Elissa stumbled home an hour ago with Michael at her heels and another death on her shoulders. She ended a man's life tonight with the knowledge and aid of two angels, and not one of us batted an eye. Tonight she will lose herself in the archangel's arms and let his touch wash away any remnants of the encounter. She will close her eyes and sleep as peacefully as any of us can manage.

The man Elissa killed tonight deserved his fate. The girl who sat on our couch a few hours ago with her scuffed sneakers and scared brown eyes was young, far too young to look so haunted. He was her father's best friend, and his wandering hands found her the first time when she was fourteen.

Her tearful confessions had never been believed. A man's

reputation was at stake, after all. Never mind hers. She shouldn't have smiled so much. Shouldn't have led him on with all that seductive politeness.

I can't believe that once upon a time I thought everyone could be saved.

How naïve I was.

In broken fingers, black eyes, and whispered stories, I learned those lessons. Some people can change. Some can be redeemed and turn away from the path of cruelty and evil. Those they wronged may never forgive, but if their hearts truly repent, they might one day find a place in Heaven.

But not all.

Some were lost long before we knew their faces, and somewhere in the bowels of Hell, there is a door with their name on it waiting.

I've seen what lies beyond those doors, and I do not grieve for the souls we send into Lucifer's hands.

But Hell isn't in Lucifer's hands anymore. I want to blame him for deserting his post and leaving the gates unguarded. When Lucifer ruled the Pit, Brielle could never have slipped inside without his awareness and made herself at home.

In those first days of darkness, when Phenex skirted around his name before saying in a broken whisper, "I don't know why Lucifer hasn't come for me" I wanted to hate him. And after uncountable days of clinging to Phenex like a life raft and listening as he poured out his memories in the blackness, I began to see a different face of the archangel I'd been taught to fear for so long.

I started to remember scraps of who Lucifer was long ago, and it became easier and easier to understand what it cost him to survive thousands upon thousands of years in the Pit.

I can't bring myself to hate him for grasping at his chance at happiness and refusing to let it be stolen from him.

But I still feel the phantom pinch of the too-tight collar

around my neck when I move too quickly. I almost envy Phenex for the ragged scar across his throat. I know the mark came from his battle with Uriel long before Brielle snared him, but I wish I had some outward mark to show what happened. A scar I could look at each day to remind myself, *Yes, this terrible thing happened. Yes, you survived. Yes, it's over.*

But we all know this ordeal is far from over. Phenex is still back in Hell, trapped inside his mind, hidden away because he feels nowhere else is safe. I can't fault him for that. Brielle tormented him for decades longer than she had me, and I feel as though I'll never quite be myself again after the pain and the darkness and the suffocating silence.

I don't have a human sharing my bed, so I spend too much of each night out here, sitting like a sentinel and awaiting the dawn.

The scars are deeper in all of us now, guilt and regret hovering too close to the surface. Elissa blames herself for Brielle's cruelties, Lucifer for Phenex's pain. I try to avoid catching Grace's eye for fear that she'll finally notice the myriad of ways I failed her family.

The grass rustles at the edge of the yard as the faintest breeze blows through, cutting the stifling humidity ever so slightly. Tomorrow will bring another woman, another tear-filled story and another broken life to piece back together.

But tonight I am restless, and I don't know why.

Phenex is across town, wrapped in the safety of Grace's pretty house and guarded by the Devil himself. My best friend is curled in the arms of her great love, finally allowing someone to chisel away the stone surrounding her heart.

How have the Fallen and the sinners found peace when I can't?

I don't begrudge any of them the scraps of joy they've found. My time in Hell taught me many things, but above all, it taught me that Heaven lied to us.

I chose my path long ago when I allied myself with Grace's family and stayed on Earth rather than returning home. And one day I awoke to find that *home* was no longer the glimmering walls of Heaven's throne room or even the tangled blooms of Eden. Home had become whatever worn-down dwelling I shared with a sullen witch, doing my tiny part to right those unanswered prayers.

The Fallen were evil. That is the line we were fed since the beginning, and we swallowed it down with no more care than a child drinking a brightly colored poison. Lucifer chose darkness and cruelty over our father's love, and those that followed him were just as bad. They deserved what became of them. *We* were the righteous.

Funny how things change.

The back door creaks behind me, and I don't need to look over my shoulder to know that Michael is the one hovering in the doorway.

"Can't sleep?"

I chuckle. Angels don't need sleep, and I'm thankful for that. I don't want to shut my eyes. The part of me that I can hide under bright smiles and frivolity in daylight claws to the surface in the dark.

That Caila is still afraid that she'll open her eyes and be back there.

I suspect Michael knows my fears. I've heard their whispered conversations, hushed voices that fall silent when I move within earshot. Elissa frets over me like a mother hen, and I'm unaccustomed to this role reversal. Usually, I'm the one tiptoeing around our fragile clients, while Elissa promises to pay them back for every tear in blood and pain. Now her wary eyes watch my every move for signs that I'm about to splinter into a thousand pieces the way Phenex has.

I wish I could.

Michael's boots scrape on the cement as he sits down

next to me. This may be the first time we've been alone together, and I'm at a loss for what to say. Michael and Elissa spend each spare moment tangled together as they relearn each other after so long apart. Seeing her so in tune with another is jarring. Even after decades of living in each other's pockets, Elissa never stopped feeling solitary, like a beast domesticated just enough to let its handlers think it was safe to touch. Underneath though, the wild still called.

She is still the same in every way that counts, but I no longer wonder if I'll awaken to a hasty goodbye note and an empty house.

Elissa is my closest friend, my *only* friend in the human sense, but I understand Michael in a way that doesn't need explanation. He's had his entire worldview ripped to shreds in the past weeks, and he's still struggling to regain his footing in the world. We're both unmoored, the ground we thought was stable heaving and swelling beneath our feet.

Grace makes throwing aside all you've ever known look simple, and I envy the surety of youth.

Michael understands what it is to feel betrayed and also to feel like the betrayer. Heaven lied to us, but casting Heaven away for humanity and the Fallen still feels like treachery.

"Do you miss it?" I ask, my voice cutting through the early morning quiet. I don't elaborate. I don't need to.

Michael shifts next to me, and I turn to look at him. He averts his eyes, the deep indigo lost in the shadows. His hands rest in his lap, his fingers flexing as though unconsciously searching for a weapon to grip. I fear Michael will always be forced to be the warrior, at least within his own mind. No amount of peace will be strong enough to wash away the remnants of the blood he shed for Heaven.

"I miss what it was," Michael whispers. "I miss who we were."

He doesn't need to speak the litany of names. I hear them on each breath. *Lucifer. Uriel. Gabriel.* I wonder how Raphael has managed to hold onto so much of himself. Lucifer fell, Uriel died, Gabriel ran. And we are what's left.

We both fall into easy silence as the sky lightens behind the silhouette of the skyscraper in the distance. *The Plaza Tower*, I realize as the light grows. Forty-five stories of nothing - abandoned, repaired, and then forgotten again. Seems fitting that this is the landmark that catches my eye tonight.

"How is he?"

I smile sadly at Michael's concern. He and Lucifer are on the long road of forgiving each other for their mutual trespasses, but Phenex is something wholly different to Michael – a Fallen creature who *chose* to follow Lucifer into the Pit.

So many didn't. Heaven splintered when Lucifer fell, even if he wasn't there to see it. Some that believed in him fought in his stead, trusting that if they brought Heaven to its knees they would sit at Lucifer's right hand.

Others saw Michael return alone with a bloody sword and haunted eyes and threw themselves on Heaven's mercy lest they meet Lucifer's same end.

Only Phenex walked away from both sides and stood at the edge, gazing down into the black depths Lucifer had disappeared into. Only Phenex stepped over the edge of his own free will.

Of all the tormented citizens of Hell, Phenex is the only one who truly chose to be there.

"That same," I answer.

It's truth and a lie all wrapped into one. I see flickers of him, mayfly short moments when he looks at me instead of through me, but each time I try to draw him out he huddles deeper into himself.

I was a trap. I was a lure.

Brielle needed us, needed our blood and our power to scratch her way into Heaven, but she didn't need us broken. Her spells subdued us, and she could have bled us dry anytime. Wrapped in those chains, weak as humans, we had no hope to stop her.

But Brielle wanted us to suffer for the crime of being angels. We all had her Nephilim lover's blood on our hands in her eyes, and she made certain we paid for it.

Phenex snapped too quickly for her liking, so she needed to bring him back. After all, what's the point of torture if your victim can't feel it?

And I made him feel again. I woke him up to more agonies.

This time, he knows better.

Michael reaches over and grips my shoulder, squeezing it softly. I pretend not to notice the slight hesitation before he touches me, as though his hand could shatter this porcelain thin veil of normalcy I wear.

"He'll come around." Michael's voice is sure. He has Elissa back. Lucifer is his brother again. Heaven may be in turmoil, but Michael's two greatest regrets have righted themselves, so the rest of the world looks just a little brighter. "He survived Hell long before Brielle came into any of our lives," he adds. "He'll come through this."

"Of course he will," I echo. The first streaks of orange slice across the sky as dawn breaks, and I want to stare at it until the light scorches my eyes and I see the brightness even when they're closed.

Phenex survived Hell at Lucifer's side and when the screams of the tormented grew to be too much he slipped away to Earth to revel with small-time sinners. Phenex lost himself in lust and gluttony, in pleasure and indolence, but loyalty always called him back.

He wasn't alone. He wasn't brutalized and left to suffer in the darkness. He didn't believe he had been forgotten.

I wouldn't have survived Hell without him, and I was what destroyed him.

3

PHENEX

She leaves us in the darkness.

Caila and I never stray more than an arm's length from each other. Every few hours or days we struggle to our feet, standing only long enough to stretch our stiff limbs as we search in vain for a more comfortable position on the bare store. But even in those moments we never take more than a step or two apart.

I finally understand the desperation humans lost at sea must feel with the cold, dead eyes of Heaven gazing down from above and the unknowable depths of the ocean below. Ship-wrecked, we cling to each other, and fear and proximity have a way of forcing intimacy in a way the outside world never can.

After we exhaust our voices and our stories, filling this chasm around us with every bright memory we can summon, we simply lie together on the unyielding ground and listen to the sound of each other's breath. Caila's head is pillowed on my chest, the sound of my heartbeat echoing in her ear as I run my fingers through the tangles of her hair, taking my time to smooth out each snarl I find.

I wonder what Heaven would think of us now.

I tilt my head, and the scar from Uriel's blade aches under the rough metal of the collar. In the moments after Grace healed me, I caught the faintest glimpse of what she truly is beneath that veil of humanity that still cloaks her. Her heart was laid bare as she summoned up powers she didn't yet understand to heal me for no other reason than because she knew I mattered to Lucifer.

What they feel for each other, it suffuses them both like oxygen or sunlight. It brought Lucifer back from death and gave Grace the strength to kill. Lost in the darkness with nothing but the press of Caila against my side to tether me to reality, I'm beginning to understand that power.

Click click click.

Every part of me goes cold.

"What is it?" Caila whispers as my arms tighten around her and my body goes rigid. Her voice fades away as the *click click click* comes closer.

Please don't.

I don't realize I said it aloud until Caila's frantic voice asking, "Please don't *what*, Phenex?" cuts through my stupor. She's so attuned to me that Caila hasn't even realized that we aren't alone.

Somehow in the last few minutes, Caila pulled me upright, and she's kneeling next to me, shaking my shoulder as she tries to bring me back to her.

"So cozy. I knew you two would get along."

Caila freezes at the unexpected sound, and I don't need vision to recognize the look of utter hopelessness her face is surely wearing. Being trapped in the darkness with nothing but our own fears is terrible enough, but having that terror made flesh is so much worse.

And now I have something to lose.

"Such a pretty picture," she continues, her low voice filling the cavern.

I struggle to my feet, pulling Caila with me, and summon up every weakened thread of divinity still running through me, even though I know it won't be enough.

Humans dream of miracles, of incurable cancers slipping into remission and frozen bodies shuddering back to life.

Angels know better.

There are no miracles. There is only power, and right now only one of us has that.

It isn't me.

"Kneel." It isn't a request, but I don't move, staring defiantly into the darkness until the collar tightens, buckling my knees and wrenching me downward. My knees hit the cold stone in the same moment Caila is ripped from me and dragged into the darkness.

I try to rise, pushing up against the pressure on my back and shoulders, but it's like trying to move a mountain. The more I fight, the more the weight bears down on me, pressing me lower until I'm crouched on my hands and knees.

A shriek cuts through the darkness, a shrill, animal sound torn from the throat of an angel who has never experienced true physical agony. Pain is an alien thing to so many angels. Even those born as warriors view it as human weakness.

What does not kill us heals, so pain is a no more than a temporary annoyance, forgotten before the wound closes.

But locked in this cell, wrapped in these chains, we are only angelic enough to stay alive, and the sounds that pour from Caila's throat are all too human.

I don't beg for her to stop or to trade places. I don't shut my ears against the sounds or retreat into my mind.

This is my punishment for finding the only escape possible. To hear every choked scream.

It goes on and on, Caila's cries eventually fading into

broken sobs and finally silence as the *click click click* retreats. The pressure on my back relents so abruptly that I pitch forward, barely catching myself before I land face-first on the ground.

I crawl toward the direction Caila was yanked, sweeping my arms across the ground in search of her.

I almost miss her in the darkness. My fingertip just grazes the bottom of her shoe, and I follow the line of her leg upward. She's sprawled on her front, and my stomach sinks as I touch her back as gently as I can, knowing what I'll find there.

Caila moans and shrinks away from the touch, and I yank my hand back. The whip. As creative as she might be in her horrors, our captor apparently likes to stick to a sequence.

And I remember every step.

Caila stays locked in blissful unconsciousness for hours as her skin knits back together. I stroke her hair and wait for her to awaken as I try not to think of what will happen to her next.

I JOLT AWAKE, squinting in the bright light.

Everything feels foreign. A knitted blanket is wrapped around my shoulders, the simple comfort of the soft cloth and the sensation of actually being *warm* is so jarring, so unfamiliar that it almost feels wrong.

Enough time can numb you to nearly anything.

The room I'm in is small, but it's a *room* and not a featureless void. I'm wedged in a tight space between a twin bed and the wall. Another blanket and a few pillows on the floor around me make the confined space almost feel like a nest.

As my eyes adjust to the light I realize that the blinding brightness is nothing more than a few strands of Christmas lights strung around the top of the room. The warm white glow lights up every corner of the room, cutting through the shadows. To me, it feels bright as day.

Where am I?

Cautiously, I unfold my body from my hiding place. Other than the bed, the only other objects of note in the room are a tiny desk, barely wider than wooden chair tucked underneath it and a bookshelf against the back wall stuffed to the brim with paperbacks.

The single window in the room is covered by a sheer curtain, but the radiance from the streetlights still filters in. It's nighttime, but that artificial yellow glow calls to me like an insect to a flame. I'll never take the light for granted again.

I take a tentative step forward, the wide planks of the wooden floor creaking under my feet as I walk around the bed to the closed door. My hand hesitates above the worn brass knob. What if this is just another new type of torture? I wake up somewhere else, somewhere with windows and comfort and *light*, and I think that I'm finally free until I touch the door.

My hand trembles when I twist the knob, but it opens easily, the oiled hinges silent.

It's only when I cross the threshold into the hallway that I recognize the house. The rubble Uriel and I left in our wake is long gone, but I'll never forget the huge black wings adorning the canvas in her living room.

I'm in Grace's house. And if I'm in the little shotgun house where the Last lays her head, the Devil is resting beside her.

He came for me after all.

It's over. It's really over.

I wait for the relief to wash over me, for the fear gripping my heart to finally loosen its hold, but all I feel is the same creeping dread telling me that *something* is coming.

I steal through the darkened house to the front door almost on autopilot, mechanically unfastening the deadbolts, and I stagger outside. I leave the door gaping open like a mouth behind me.

I stare at the front steps for too long, my brain barely able to comprehend the mundane scene before me. The ginger cat is absent from its usual perch, no doubt engaging in whatever nocturnal prowling cats do. The potted plants lining the steps look a bit scorched around the edges, but it's all so deceptively normal and human that my brain feels overloaded.

I let my feet carry me those last few steps out into the empty street and I crane my neck upward to gaze at the stars. There is no wide expanse of sky in New Orleans. Buildings hem in the span of Heaven and light pollution dampens the glow of the stars, but *they're real*. It's real.

I'm out.

So why do I still feel as though I'm waiting for the snare to snap closed?

I start walking down the empty street. I have no destination in mind, no plan beyond feeling the humid heat of the night on my skin and taking a step without the metallic clink of the chain following me. The night is mostly still, but the lightest breeze blows across my face, that tiny movement so different than the stale air of the tomb that I skid to a stop to revel in the sensation.

For the first time, I glance down at my clothes. The ruined suit is long gone, the scraps of linen soaked in blood and filth tossed away by my saviors. I hope they burned it. The black t-shirt and lounge pants are a bit too large for my frame, the size and the fine weave of the fabric telling me all I need to know. Lucifer. He and the Last freed me and brought me into their home.

They saved me.

Snatches of memories tug at me. Pale hair. Smoke. Golden opulence consumed by flames.

Pale hair. Soft skin that somehow still smelled of flowers. Slender fingers clinging to my own.

Caila.

Where is she?

Cold dread pours over me at the possibility that Caila might still be trapped. Grace's kind heart would never allow them to leave another behind, but if we were separated. . . I dig at my memory, but the gaps are chasms.

I turn back toward the house, needing answers far more than I need the open air. I've barely gone two steps when I catch the scent of rot on the breeze. Every part of me tenses. This is no trashcan overturned by stray dogs or a restaurant dumpster filled with the leavings of Happy Hour. This is decay and corruption. This is brimstone.

I may be free of Hell, but some part of Hell has followed.

I fight past every sense that tells me to run back into the safety of Grace's house and the small, sheltered nook I hid myself in. I am an angel. I will not bar the door and let myself be cowed again. I turn and walk back toward the city center. The stench grows stronger with every step until I turn a corner and come across the creature kneeling in the crosswalk.

Its head snaps up when it sees me. Under the glare of the streetlight, its skin is the color of oil-stained leather, cracked and worn with age. Slowly it unfolds from its crouch to stand more or less upright. Beneath the bright glow of the artificial light, it's hard to imagine this thing was ever human, but eons upon eons of torment in Hell warps the souls into their true visage.

That's what the humans always get wrong. Hell doesn't last forever. It feels like forever, but one day when the very last shred of who you were has been chipped away the door to your cell opens, and this is what exits.

"Demon." I spread my wings, hiding my flinch at the memory of the thin bones snapping, and I take a menacing step forward. In Hell, the lower demons gave the Fallen a wide berth, and this is just a foot soldier, a creature filled with nothing but the mindless desire to manufacture torment and chaos.

"Demon," it parrots back, baring jagged teeth the color of old blood. Its voice is a hollow mimic of my own, and I know its kind. In Hell it whispers a soul's own thoughts back to it, subtly twisting the words until their own mind drives them mad.

It has no speech of its own, but I can feel its hunger. It barely spares my wings a glance, the power of an angel forgotten at the prospect of so many ripe, undamaged minds.

It won't go quietly.

"You forget your place," I spit. Seeing this. . . *thing* walking the streets of Earth is an affront to everything Heaven once stood for. This is worse than Uriel trapping the souls of the damned on Earth. Evil and psychotic they might have been, but they were still human at their core. The wanton destruction those souls created in just a few days will pale if more of Hell's darkest creations start clawing through the gates.

The demon tilts his head, regarding me silently like a curious dog. Then it smiles, leathery black lips twisting back from the mottled teeth in a garish grin. I barely notice the twitch of its long fingers before it's lashing out at me.

The demon launches itself at me. The claw-tipped fingers rake a trio of gouges down my cheek, but I hardly feel them. The creature is in a frenzy, its teeth snapping inches from my throat as I push it off. It's like fighting an animal, and I reach to my side for my blade before realizing I'm unarmed.

The demon darts just out of reach, pausing as it surveys my lack of weapon with another hideous smile.

It isn't afraid.

It should be.

I'm not going back.

This time when the demon runs toward me, claws and teeth bared, I'm ready.

My fist catches it in the chest, and I feel bone give way beneath the punch. The demon drops like a stone, a wet wheeze slipping from its throat as it tries to breathe through the shards of bone embedded in its lungs.

A quick snap of its neck would end it now, weaponless or not, but the sting of the cuts on my face is too familiar, and the stenches of blood and decay and Hell are too thick in my nose to be pushed aside.

It's little more than an animal. Angels, even the Fallen, should know mercy. I should end it quickly, but I still hear my own screams, *Caila's* screams, echoing in my ears. I feel her heartbeat fluttering against mine, hummingbird fast with fear, and the one who caused it all isn't here to feel my vengeance.

But a piece of Hell is.

I grab the creature by the back of its neck and haul it upward, making sure it gets a good look at the last face it will ever see, my own vision lost behind a red haze.

There will be more blood spilled tonight, and for once, it won't be mine.

4

CAILA

The sun still hasn't crested over the roofline when Michael leaves me to my thoughts to reclaim his spot in Elissa's bed. The streets are still largely empty, though the noise of the day is starting, the hum of activity as the humans begin their day rising with the dawn.

I can't pretend my thoughts are anywhere but at Phenex's side. When he wakes up, *if* he wakes up, he could very well hate me. Brielle turned us both into weapons against the other, and the memories of furtive touches in the darkness as we fought to retain the precious threads of our sanity might not be something he wants to relive.

I could have been anyone. *He* could have been anyone.

But fate and Brielle locked us together, and until his own words send me away, I have to try.

The flight across town is quick, my wings cutting through the lightening sky with ease, and in the air, my blackest memories fade like wisps of smoke. There is nothing to fear in the wind and the skies. The updrafts catch my feathers, and I wheel a bit higher letting the utter freedom wash away my dark thoughts.

Almost too quickly I arrive at Grace's house, and when I land by her front steps those glorious moments of happiness are snuffed out like a candle doused in icy water.

The front door gapes open, creaking slightly on its hinge as the breeze blows it back and forth.

The house is still, the rooms silent and dark, and as I cross the threshold I feel the familiar whisper of magic as the wards Elissa enrobed the house in recognize me. The protections on the house are intact, and nothing could have made it through those without alerting the house's other occupants.

The door to Phenex's room hangs open, and I duck my head inside to confirm what I already know.

He's gone.

I rush back outside and take to the air, all thoughts of alerting the others forgotten in my desperate dash to *find him*.

I barrel through the skies, making a sweeping circle to the south, my eyes scanning the streets below. Thoughts of Phenex wandering the streets while still trapped in the Hell of his own mind flood me, and I'm so intent on my own worries that I nearly miss him. He's barely half a mile from the house, standing alone next to a streetlight and swaying on his bare feet.

Even from a distance, the scene looks *wrong*.

I land a few feet behind him and take in the horror before me.

The thick scent of blood fills the air, but even the heavy taste of copper hanging in the humid air isn't enough to cover the stink of the dead demon at his feet. The creature is a mess of twisted limbs and ruptured meat, a testament to angelic strength and rage made flesh.

I circle Phenex slowly, taking care to keep a few feet back from him. His arms are spattered with gore up to his elbows, the red-black of the demon's blood already drying on his skin. When his profile comes into view I see three streaks of blood across his face, the gouges that caused them nearly healed.

He looks dazed, even shocked by his own strength and actions but he blinks his eyes and *looks* at me.

Not through me.

I take a step closer, and I still expect him to recoil, to curl back into himself the way he has each time one of us has moved too quickly or spoken too loud.

"Phenex?" My voice cracks under the weight of his name. There's so much hope in those two syllables.

Phenex blinks again and takes a hesitating step closer to me. "Caila?" He stumbles over my name, his voice raw as gravel from lack of use. "Are you here?" He stops, glancing wildly around us as though he's expecting the chains to tighten again. "Is this real?"

"I'm here. It's real," I whisper, closing the last steps between us. I reach out and take one of his hands in mine. His skin is sticky with the demon's drying blood, and I feel the tiny tremors in his muscles as he tries to keep from pulling away.

Does he even remember the last time he was touched for any reason but to cause pain?

"It's over," I finish, letting go of his hand before I can overwhelm him even further.

"No, it's not." His voice is haunted as he stares down at the body at our feet. Already the demon is crumbling to ash, and in a few more minutes nothing will remain of its corpse beyond a mound of blackened dust and a few rusty stains on the concrete.

"It's not over," Phenex repeats, "More are coming."

PHENEX SITS on one of the wooden chairs tucked against

Grace's heavy kitchen table, fidgeting under the well-meaning scrutiny as five pairs of eyes try and fail to look anywhere but at him.

The small room is crowded. Grace fumbles with a coffeemaker, her fingers still clumsy with sleep. Her grey eyes dart from Lucifer to Phenex and back again. She nudges Michael, arching one eyebrow as if to silently ask the archangel *what now?*

Michael shrugs his shoulders. He has no more insight into his brother's strange dynamic with Phenex than the rest of us do, though I don't think I'm imagining the spark of guilty jealousy in Michael's face when he looks at the man who replaced him as Lucifer's closest confidant and friend.

Elissa sits perched on the kitchen counter, leaning against Michael's bulk as she struggles to snap herself back into war mode. Her dark hair is tied up in a hasty ponytail, the chestnut tendrils falling around her face giving her a softer look than I'm used to.

Four hours of sleep wasn't nearly enough to chase the shadows from around her eyes, but I think she expected this far more than the rest of us. Elissa hasn't allowed herself more than a momentary respite after Brielle. She's spent this honeymoon period with Michael perpetually on edge, and under the exhaustion, she looks almost grateful that the other shoe has finally dropped.

Grace hands her a steaming cup of coffee, and she smiles gratefully, gulping down the scorching drink as we all wait for this tangled night to unravel.

Lucifer hovers too close to Phenex's chair, looking like he desperately wants to rip *someone* apart. For a moment I almost wish Brielle was still alive so that we could let Lucifer at her. Grace squeezes his arm and he relaxes almost imperceptibly before snapping his attention back to Phenex.

Even Grace's presence isn't enough to calm the Devil now.

In slow, halting words Phenex recounts the last few hours – the confusion of waking up in an unfamiliar room, wandering through the house in the quiet of the night before finding his way to the street, and the elation of open air. More than anything, I hear what he's leaving out.

I thought I was still back there. I thought it wasn't real. Some part of me still *thinks that.*

Phenex keeps his eyes downcast, staring far too intently at the worn wood of the table, tracing the ripples and lines of the grain with a bloodstained fingertip. I'd tried to fuss over him, checking him needlessly for injuries hidden under the demon blood, and he'd shrugged off my touch. It was all too much. I understood, but it still stung.

"It was a soldier demon," he finishes, "Nothing special, but if they can find their way out of Hell you know more will follow. *Worse* will follow."

"Did it know who you are?" Lucifer's voice is clipped, the anger barely restrained. He circles around the table, pacing as much as he's able to in the cramped space the room affords him. When Phenex nods, Lucifer clenches both fists and turns his back to him, nearly vibrating with repressed fury at the insult.

"That demon knew who you were, and it still attacked you." It isn't a question.

"You knew this could happen when you left."

Michael's quiet voice rings out through the edgy stillness of the room. Lucifer whirls to face him, his lips curled back over his teeth, and just like that these last few weeks of brotherly affection seem forgotten. "Do you think I expected this?" he snaps.

Michael isn't backing down from his brother's ire. "Did you think they would all just continue to fall in line if you left for good?" He takes a step closer to Lucifer, drawing himself up to his considerable height and the tension in the room ratchets up another level. Grace and Elissa both look ready to intercede, but this is far from the first time Michael and Lucifer have argued in the past weeks.

And for once, neither of them is in the wrong.

Michael continues without pausing for breath, and this might be the most I've ever heard the stoic angel speak. "You know far better than I do about the infighting and jockeying for favor in Hell. You left a power vacuum behind, Lucifer." He spares a glance at Phenex. "You both did. What did you expect would happen?"

Caught between the two immovable archangels, Phenex seems to shrink even more into himself. It's easy to forget that this subdued creature served as Lucifer's right hand in Hell for so many years.

Subdued, but not broken. Not shattered as we all thought.

A dead demon shouldn't make me hopeful, but it does.

"And what was I supposed to do?" Lucifer's voice has dropped to barely above a whisper, but the quiet tone leaves no room for argument. "I did my time. I suffered for *eons*," he snarls, his voice rising. "I thought you agreed that my sentence was long enough, brother."

Michael flinches. It's a low blow, and Lucifer knows it, but Michael doesn't stop pushing. "Soldier demons are nothing," he says, every inch Heaven's greatest warrior. "With a weapon, even Grace could kill one, but you know it won't stop with them."

"They wouldn't dare."

"You're too old to be naïve, brother," Michael shoots back. "They have already dared." Michael sighs, centuries of battle fatigue in that exhalation. A few quiet weeks certainly aren't enough to erase that. "Those demons are just scouts. If there's one, there will be more, and one of them will make it back to report."

Lucifer slams his palm against the table, making Phenex jolt backward. The old wood creaks but doesn't splinter as the archangel tries to hold his bubbling rage in check. As abruptly as it came on, Lucifer's barely contained anger melts into cold calculation. "We need to find the rifts Brielle opened and seal them before anything else gets through." Lucifer slips back into the mantle of cunning general with ease.

Across the room, Elissa is sitting ramrod straight, already mentally preparing to throw herself on the front lines of a war she blames herself for.

"They won't just be demons." Every word still seems like a struggle for Phenex, fighting against the impulse to crawl back into the safety of his own mind. His voice is hushed, but we all fall silent as he speaks. "The other Fallen will be coming, and they'll make what Uriel did to this city look like Mardi Gras." Phenex stands up. Caught between Michael and Lucifer he looks small, but streaked with blood, he looks far from weak.

Not broken. Not at all.

"If a scout will attack your right hand without fear, that means they aren't worried about retaliation from you anymore." Phenex pushes past Lucifer, and the archangel makes no move to stop him.

Phenex pauses in the mouth of the darkened hallway to add, "They'll be coming for all of us, but they'll be coming for you the most." He walks away, and a moment later the front door opens and then slams shut.

I start to follow, but Lucifer shakes his head. "Let him go. He's right." Lucifer sighs heavily, sinking down on the chair Phenex vacated. "I have a few ideas of who will be the first in line to challenge me. Malphas. Belial. Abaddon. There are others that will claw their way to the surface just for the chance to wreak their own flavor of havoc. I certainly wouldn't put it past the Horsemen to try to find their way out."

Lucifer glances up at Elissa. "The wards on this house and your own? Double them." Elissa opens her mouth, bristling at any implication that her wards aren't already enough to protect us, but Lucifer silences her with a raised hand. "Whatever you think you've done, it's not enough. These are the worst of the Fallen. Do you think they have scruples that demand a fair fight?"

Lucifer falls silent, mulling over his next words for far longer than is comfortable. "Is there any possibility at all that the necromancer is alive?"

Elissa nods stiffly. None of us want to believe that Brielle could have survived Michael's blade and the fire, but she pulled herself from the ashes once before. This was a woman who survived fire and Heavenly blades once already, to say nothing of ripping her way into Hell and snaring two angels.

"If she is alive, she's gone to ground," Elissa replies. "We won't find her unless she wants to be found."

"Then we're on our own." Lucifer turns to me, his dark eyes demanding answers. "You were there with him. I haven't pushed either of you, but none of us have the luxury of being coddled anymore." Lucifer grabs my wrist, and I hold his gaze, keeping my arm steady beneath his grasp. "Is he ready to fight?" he grinds out, enunciating every word as his eyes bore into mine. "Are you?"

"Yes," I answer, but I can't keep the stammer from my voice.

Lucifer releases my arm, and I take a quick step backward. He notices. "No, you're not." Lucifer stands up and stalks closer. He crowds me, and I don't even realize that I've been backing away from him until my back hits the wall. "You know I won't harm you, but still you recoil. You're safer in this room than anywhere else on this planet, and yet you hide still." One arm shoots forward to grip the doorjamb, penning me in.

"Lucifer, back off!" Elissa snarls, but the Devil pays her no mind.

"If you can't handle this, you need to return to Heaven." Lucifer's voice softens. "Despite the company you keep, you aren't Fallen. You can still go back."

"No." My voice doesn't waver on that word in the slightest, and Lucifer drops his arm as realization slowly filters across his face.

"Does he know?" he asks. At my confused look, he lets out a bitter chuckle. "Of course not. *You* don't even know. What a group we make."

"Lucifer." Grace doesn't say anything but his name, but the strain we're all feeling loosens a fraction. I meet Grace's eyes over Lucifer's shoulder, and I see nothing but pure compassion filling their grey depths. She is Serafine's iron will, Marianne's stubbornness, and Will's kind heart all wrapped into one, and compassion is the last thing I deserve from her after failing her entire family.

I look away.

Lucifer answers Grace without looking at her, the bite dropping from his voice. "We can't afford a weak link, no matter who they are. Not now." Lucifer steps back from me. I know he won't stop me if I try to walk away now, but I stay rooted to the spot. "If one of you is facing down Asmodeus or Abaddon or *any* of them, do you think you'll get a second chance if you freeze?"

I don't answer. Everyone in the room knows that he's right.

PHENEX IS SITTING on Grace's front steps, staring out at the early morning traffic barreling down the road. The ginger tabby cat lolls in his lap, baring the paler gold of its belly to Phenex's idly stroking hand.

"It's all so bright. How did you get used to it again?"

"I don't think I ever will," I reply, sitting down beside him. The wet washcloth in my hand drips cool water down my arm, and I lean closer, wiping the rusty streaks off his cheek before taking his hand and washing away the flakes of dried blood still clinging to his skin.

The cat watches us both with placid green eyes, but it's Phenex's gaze that I'm intently aware of as I cleanse his skin. When the last trace of the demon is gone from his hand I switch to the other, keeping my eyes focused on my task instead of his questioning blue eyes. Methodically, I spread his fingers, the soft fabric finding where the deep red streaks have dried around his fingernails and the creases of his knuckles.

He did this for me back in Hell, as best as he was able. We had no water, had nothing resembling a clean towel, but I remember him tearing off strips of his shirt and wrapping my broken fingers. *"It hurts less if they can heal correctly,"* he murmured, and I bit my lip until I tasted blood to keep from crying out as he set the broken bones because I knew I wasn't the only one suffering.

"Caila." Phenex's other hand covers mine, stilling my movements.

"I'm sorry," I whisper.

"For what?" Phenex lets go of my hands and brushes one finger across my cheek, wiping away the moisture. I hadn't even realized I was crying.

"For making it worse. For being something she could use against you." The words tumble out of me before I can stop them.

"You have nothing to be sorry for," Phenex answers.

There's no hesitation in his voice. No regret. "Brielle did this, not you." He tucks a strand of hair behind my ear, the touch lingering on my skin. "You brought me back. You gave me a reason to try to fight until it was all just *too much*-" His voice breaks off, and I know what memory his mind is trying to push to the surface.

I WAKE up wrapped in his arms. Phenex's skin pressed against mine is the only thing that's real other than the pain and the cold, oppressive darkness. I've lost track of the torture I've endured. Days or weeks ago, Phenex let it slip that he knew what was coming. Our captor wasn't changing her routine, and he'd already experienced every lash and every burn in sequence.

I begged him to warn me, to prepare me for what was coming, but he refused.

"Not knowing was better," he said.

She came and went and left me whole, the anticipation of torment almost crueler than its actuality, and something in me finally snaps. I cling to Phenex in the darkness, soaking his chest with my tears and pleading for it to just be *over*.

"I just want to feel something besides the cold."

I can't say who seeks who, but somewhere in the darkness, our lips meet. His are dry and cracked, bitten raw from hiding his reactions from our jailer and from me. We both freeze at that first touch, and in the light of day, this would be madness.

In the light of day, we would belong to Hell and Heaven.

But in the unyielding blackness we have nothing but each other, and when Phenex's mouth parts beneath mine, I feel just the tiniest bit alive again.

Once the dam between us breaks, we can't get close

enough. Phenex hauls me onto his lap, and my hands skate over his chest, feeling the worn remnants of his suit beneath my palms, innumerable slashes and rends in the blood-stiffened fabric.

He pulls back, barely breaking the kiss, and I feel the ghost of his breath across my lips.

He doesn't ask if this is what I want or whisper noble words to give me an out. He says nothing at all.

Instead, his lips find mine again in the inky darkness, and his hands tighten around my waist, pulling me closer.

I lose myself in sensation. In our blindness, there is nothing but touch and taste and sound. My ears focus on the ragged noise of Phenex's breath as I kiss his jaw. I feel his pulse beneath my lips, fluttering below his skin like a trapped bird.

For a second, I almost forget.

Then I slide my lips downward and meet the smooth iron of the collar, and it douses my fantasy like a shock of cold water.

I think we'll die here.

The thought is almost freeing. We've both long since lost any hope of escape or rescue. Once we clung to the idea that our captor had plans for us beyond perpetual torment, but her continued silence has even withered that weak belief.

No, there will be nothing but darkness and pain until she grows bored and ends us.

So why not grasp at whatever scraps of comfort we can find?

My movements stilled when I touched that grim reminder of our captivity. Of course, Phenex notices. One of his hands leaves my waist to find my hand in the darkness, tangling our fingers together and bringing them to his lips.

Without words, Phenex understands.

This is all we have.

Soon enough the sharp click of her heels will echo on the stone, signaling more pain or more psychological torture.

There is no more Heaven for me. There is just this.

I kiss him again, and there's nothing tentative anymore. I think I startle him a bit with my vehemence. Sprawled flat on his back on the rigid stone floor of our prison, Phenex can't be comfortable, but the lack of cushioning is the last thing on either of our minds.

The chains clatter unnoticed against the floor as we devour each other. Is this what the damned souls go through? Forgetting their lives, their dreams, their very names until nothing is left but animal instincts?

My garrison would scorn me for this. Uriel would cast me out. But if I'm truly honest, I set myself adrift long ago.

Elissa would understand. She always understood.

I might not be truly Fallen yet, but I'm more of a part of Lucifer's world than I am of Heaven.

I tug at Phenex's shirt, unfastening the buttons with more care than is needed with our already ruined clothing. When I feel the fabric part I run my hands across the planes of his chest. The slow thump of his heartbeat quickens under my fingertips, and his hips rock against mine as we both search for more contact.

"Caila," his voice is hardly even a whisper, just a bare exhalation that forms the syllables of my name.

In that moment, I almost love him.

I want more. I want to feel every inch of his skin against mine, heat and friction chasing away the cold that has seeped into my bones. I want to tear off the dirty rags clothing my body that once upon a time called itself a dress, but I can almost feel her eyes watching us. The darkness may hide us from each other, but not her. So I keep my meager armor.

Phenex's free hand toys with the hem of my skirt. Under

the layers of grime and blood and ash, it's pale blue, the color of the highest reaches of the skies. I wonder if he remembers.

"Phenex." I don't know what I'm asking for. His heart pounds beneath my hand, and I press my body closer, trapping that hand between us. I count time with each pulse against my palm, and I ache for him.

"Phenex," I repeat, and he silences me with another kiss. Even those whispers are too much, too loud, and we fall back into silence.

Phenex's hands trail across my body, broadly telegraphing every movement as they skim down my back. He pauses at each vertebra, counting the bones like a rosary.

He touches me like he's afraid I'll shatter around him, as though we both aren't already broken beyond repair.

I shift against him and feel his hardness pressing against my thigh and his heart throbbing under my hand.

Alive.

Real.

I squirm on top of him, and he bites back a groan at my movement.

I kiss him and let him feel the smile on my lips.

I free my trapped hand, and we're both in a frenzy as we fumble with zippers and buttons. His hands find their way beneath my skirt, and the sound of ripping fabric cuts through the quiet as the impractical piece of silk gives way.

I sit up, shivering as Phenex's fingertips brush the sensitive skin of my inner thigh. I imagine another life where we could take our time, learning each other until we forget Heaven and Hell and anything but our own pleasure.

Instead, I feel the cold stone under my knees, as I sink down onto him.

The pleasure catches us both by surprise. Phenex's arms snake around me as he sits up, crushing me against his chest as his hips find my rhythm. I pepper kisses across his face, pressing my lips to his cheekbones, his eyelids, anywhere I can touch.

His arms have a vice-grip around my waist as though he's the only thing tethering me here. The chains clink against each other in time with our movements, and I can almost imagine the sound is the hollow clank of the copper pipes our neighbor in New Orleans hung from her porch to keep bad spirits from her door.

Phenex buries his face in my neck and breathes the Enochian words into my neck like secrets. *Beautiful* and *beloved* and *I'm so sorry.* Fallen or not, he will always be an angel first.

We both need to remember that.

I gasp, the sound wrenched from somewhere deep within me, and my fingers dig into Phenex's shoulders as our pace grows more frantic. Silence and discretion, fear and loss fall away. There's nothing but the building pleasure between us, the sweet slide of his length inside me.

Phenex seals his mouth over mine, swallowing the cry that would echo through the cell as I come apart around him. My eyes fall shut as I ride the waves of bliss, and I can almost see stars on the inside of my eyelids.

A few heartbeats later Phenex shudders against me, his moan of release lost in my mouth.

The stone is no softer when we lay beside each other, our breathing still ragged as reverberations of pleasure travel across our skin. The air hasn't grown warmer. Soon enough, the cold will seep back into us, and I tuck myself closer around Phenex. His lips brush the top of my head, and I tell myself that the reason we're both trembling is aftershocks and our sweaty skin cooling on the damp ground.

His heart thumps beneath my ear, and I know I'm lying.

5

PHENEX

I've known Lucifer for enough years to sense when he's aching for a fight.

Grace's kitchen has long since been commandeered as our war room. Maps of the city are spread across her kitchen table, spilling off the edge of the wooden surface like falling leaves. Lucifer and Michael huddle over the pages, bickering like children over the likeliest location of the first rift.

"We should go back to whatever remains of that mansion," Michael argues, poking a spot on the map hard enough to wrinkle the paper.

Lucifer shakes his head. "Do you think she'd want a door to Hell close to that pretty little palace of hers? That was her fortress against Heaven *and* Hell. Whatever rift she used most won't be anywhere close."

I remember the mansion in flashes and fragments. A blur of gold and white. The sting of the collar tightening around my neck. The scent of smoke and flames. That psychotic bitch holding a knife to Caila's throat.

Hurting her felt good. Too good. But even the glory of

finally getting a taste of vengeance wasn't enough to keep the numbness at bay. As the fire ate through the walls, I slipped away again.

We all survived the day, but the Lucifer I know would never consider that fight a win. Not with an unknown number of doors to Hell gaping open and inviting the worst of the worst to come out and play.

It's beginning to feel as though we've been caught in the cycle of reacting since we came topside. Uriel set the stage, and we almost *died*. Tens of thousands of years of surviving Hell and all its miseries, and we both almost bled out on the floor of a hotel lobby. We would have if Lucifer's little blonde hadn't wrenched us back from the brink of death.

Grace hovers at the periphery of the room, leaning against the kitchen counter and peppering the two archangels with possible locations within the city. It's easy to forget that until a few weeks ago she thought she was just another human.

As for Brielle, I didn't even know her name until a few hours ago, and even after all they've seen, I think the archangels don't know everything she's capable of.

She was human once too.

And then there's Elissa. She abandoned the crowded kitchen and laid claim to the living room, spreading the tools of her trade across Grace's new coffee table. The worn spellbooks look strange on the smooth black-lacquered wood, but at least this one won't shatter into a thousand pieces under an angelic brawl.

The pungent scent of burning herbs weaves through the house as Elissa strengthens the wards, and the tingle of magic across my skin relaxes me the tiniest increment.

The sarcastic, sharp-tongued woman is one of the most powerful witches I've ever come across, and she somehow managed to lay claim to Michael's heart. Lucifer's parting gift of immortality gave her years to hone her skill that didn't require selling off parts of herself to whatever demons were buying, but I doubt even she would have the raw power needed to rip her way into the Pit.

We're outgunned, and deep down we all know it.

I shouldn't be surprised that Hell wouldn't let any of us off easy.

I always hated it there.

It's not surprising, of course. Hell was made to be a torment to *everyone*, not just the damned souls. The Fallen that follow as vassals under Lucifer's rule allowed themselves be changed into something so far removed from Heaven's grace to be unrecognizable. They let their basest impulses roam free in Hell, and it turned them into something no better than the sinners they guarded.

I was different.

I hated the ugliness of Hell and the wanton malice of its citizens. Those souls that end up there deserve it. There are no mistakes in Hell, no clerical errors where an innocent takes a wrong turn and ends up on the hills of Golgotha. The souls we stand sentry over are blackened long before they reach our door, but I could never allow myself to revel in that darkness just to punish them.

In Hell, cruelties stack upon cruelties, and the angels I once called brothers and sisters in Heaven became twisted into something I didn't recognize.

They are still angels, and somewhere in the depths of their blackened souls, they remember that. Their faces still hold every trace of the beauty our Father gave them, but they're all poisoned flowers.

And they hate humanity. Reviling the souls in our care is easy. Watching an endless loop of sins would drown anyone's pity, but to the rest of the Fallen, there is no difference between an innocent and guilty soul.

There are only souls that haven't sinned *yet*.

For centuries, I ignored their sneers at my back. How could they begin to understand me? Hell wasn't a punishment I was forced into. Our Father didn't toss me into perdition for the crime of asking too many questions or choosing the wrong side in the war. I took that first step into the Pit willingly, and for so many years, it was worth what I lost.

Hell was freedom from living underneath the stifling yoke of Heaven. I never hated the humans. I envied their reckless freedoms, and I threw myself into every vice they had to offer. I tasted each liberty that a good little angel would deny himself, and I guzzled it down. Wine, women, and song were all I desired.

I could have left Hell behind many times.

Heaven was forbidden to me, but I wasn't trapped in Hell due to divine punishment. I could come and go as I pleased, and the wide world beckoned me with open arms. I let myself give in to the thrall of humanity again and again and again over the centuries, but I always found my way back to Hell.

To Lucifer.

I hated Hell, but I never hated him.

In the Pit, I served as Lucifer's right hand, the only one he could trust without reservations. As long as he remained buried under the mountain of humanity's growing sins, I couldn't leave him behind to rot.

I grew to hate Hell more and more, but I never forgot I was an angel.

I was the Devil's second in command. I walked the world without fear until I woke up with a chain around my neck. Then I knew nothing but darkness and agony until that sliver of light Caila brought with her snapped me back to reality and gave me hope.

One would think that I more than anyone would know the treacherous danger of hope.

After so long in the night, I sprinted toward her sun, not caring if it would consume me in the end.

I WAKE UP ALONE.

I'm not surprised.

She knows we sought comfort in each other, and comfort can't be allowed in this place.

"Caila?"

The darkness swallows up my voice, and I get to my feet. I pick a direction at random and walk blindly. The chain scrapes along the floor, trailing behind me like a metallic serpent.

How fitting. Hadn't I tasted the forbidden fruit, after all?

The collar tightens as I reach the end of the tether, and I stand frozen for a moment before yelling, "CAILA" into the void.

Silence.

I hang my head as the realization that I'll probably never see her again washes over me. I'm alone again, with nothing but the days and nights of pain to look forward to.

And somewhere in another cell where I can't reach her, Caila is enduring the same.

I sit down on the stone floor, and I don't move for a long time.

THE BRIGHTNESS that flares through the room jolts me to life. Black spots swim across my eyes as my vision struggles to acclimate after so long in darkness. The light doesn't fill the room and show me anything as comforting as walls or a door.

The blurred space is still little more than a bubble of light in the inky void I'm trapped inside.

Despite it all, I can't contain the tiny ember of hope. The last light I saw brought me Caila. Maybe, just maybe, this will bring her back.

When my eyes finally focus on the tall form standing before me it's not the haughty face of our captor staring down at me. It's not sweet Caila, battered and afraid but still alive.

It's Lucifer.

He came. He finally came for me.

"Lucifer!" I struggle to my feet, forgetting the chain and the collar and the utter hopelessness I'd been so close to drowning in. All that matters is Lucifer has come for me. He'll make her pay, and this will be over.

"I knew you wouldn't forget me."

"No Phenex, I don't *forget*."

I freeze mid-step at the coldness in his voice, dragging my gaze upward to meet the chilling black of his eyes. There's no familiarity, no camaraderie born of years by his side. His eyes are the same blank darkness as the void surrounding us.

No. No no no no not him. Not Lucifer.

Lucifer moves closer, and I feel like prey caught in the open as a predator stalks closer.

I want to run.

I've seen Lucifer's rages. I watched him, blood-soaked and wrathful in the earliest days of Hell when the Horsemen rode free and the sons of men trembled at his name. I looked him in the face after trading his beloved to Michael for a chance to return to Heaven.

I've never been afraid of him before.

Lucifer smiles, and it's the grin of the Devil that stares down at me. Thousands of years of memories fall away like dust.

I'm just another soul strapped to the rack.

"I never forget, Phenex," he purrs. His hand trails down my neck, pausing at the collar. Underneath the metal, my scar throbs.

"Kneel."

I don't hesitate. I drop gracelessly to my knees, unable to hide the tremors across my body under Lucifer's harsh gaze.

This amuses him, and he chuckles darkly, his hand resting on the top of my head like I'm his well-trained pet. "Good boy. You always did know your place."

This isn't him, some distant corner of my mind protests. *This isn't Lucifer.*

"You're not Lucifer," I stammer. I dare to tilt my head up, searching his face for any cracks that would tell me this is just another trick of Hell.

This was always the easiest way to break a soul. Have their tormenter wear a familiar face and their hope dies on the vine, leaving nothing but a broken husk.

It's a trick, I tell myself, and years ago I might have believed it, but it's been too much for too long.

"Am I?" Lucifer asks. The toe of his shoe catches me in the ribs, and I feel the bones snap under the blow. It's nowhere close to the top of the list of pain that I've endured here, but it catches me by surprise. I end up sprawled on my back, gasping for air as each breath grinds my broken ribs together. Another kick catches me in the same spot, and I curl around myself, each movement causing more agony.

"You always were weak, Phenex. It's amazing I put up with you for as long as I did, but any port in the storm." The blows rain down across my body, archangel strength bruising flesh and cracking bones, and it's so much worse than the silent, clinical torture of the past.

It's not him, but that doesn't matter anymore.

I don't even realize that I've wrapped my wings around

my body in an unconscious attempt to shield myself until I feel the first wing bone shatter. Lucifer buries his hands in my feathers, and the delicate flight bones splinter beneath his grasp.

I don't have it in me to scream anymore. The darkness swims at the edge of my vision, welcoming me to its dead, numb embrace.

This time, I don't fight.

I'm sorry Caila, I whisper as I'm pulled under.

"I KNOW where we need to go."

Elissa stands in the doorway, a charred scrap of black fabric clutched in her hand. Five sets of eyes turn to her. "Luckily you weren't exactly neat when you took out that demon," she says, plucking the pen from Michael's hand and circling Marais Street, just beyond the St Louis Cemetery.

"Blood always leaves a trail, doesn't it?" Lucifer asks.

Elissa nods stiffly, her mouth a tight line. The shadows under her eyes haven't faded, and I haven't missed the evasive looks she gives to Caila and myself when she thinks we aren't paying attention.

I know guilt, however misplaced, when I see it.

"I still don't know how many rifts we have to deal with, but at least this will be a start," she adds.

Lucifer hasn't looked up from the crooked circle she drew on the map, the tense line of his shoulders telegraphing his thoughts as easily as if he spoke them aloud.

A doorway back to Hell, the place he never wanted to return to.

One little push and he could end up back there. Any of us could.

THE RIFT IS a wound in the air.

Tucked in an alleyway off a side street, it pulses about a yard above the ground, the jagged edges glowing the faded russet shade of old blood. As we watch, the rift widens, and one long, clawed arm reaches through, followed a moment later by another as it vomits another demon into the world. The creature doesn't notice us at first, turning back to the opening as more and more of its fellows are disgorged into the world.

I was right.

A scout made it back, and this is just the first wave.

I hate being right.

I lose count after a dozen or so. The creatures clamber over each other, snarling and hissing as they fight to be the first to escape out into this world of sunlight and fresh air and souls ripe for the taking.

We're crowded at the mouth of the alley, each of us waiting for Lucifer's signal to attack. Beside me, Elissa stands frozen, an unnatural stillness that has little to do with obediently awaiting orders and everything to do with shock at what she's witnessing.

It's easy to think of Hell as just a metaphor if you haven't seen it with your own eyes, even for someone such as her. Elissa's ice-blue eyes are wide and unblinking she stares at the tear in the thin membrane separating our worlds and the misshapen creatures pushing their way out in a gruesome parody of birth.

"What do we do?" Caila whispers, trying to snap Elissa back to herself. We're all armed, strapped to the hilt with Heaven and Hell forged blades, magic and angelic power simmering under our skins, but we're already outnumbered and every heartbeat that passes brings more demons through the rift.

Those that have already made it through claw at the edge of the rift, their animalistic minds focused only on letting more and more of their brethren through. The magic shudders under their onslaught, the edges of the opening glowing a deeper crimson.

And then the first notices us.

It's another soldier demon, larger than the one I fought. It growls low in its throat when it sees us, and a dozen others turn away from the rift at the noise. Blackened lips pull back from jagged teeth as they all fix us with garish smiles.

The temperature in the still air of the alley hovers near the triple-digit mark, thick with humidity, but when the first demon takes a slow step forward all I can feel is the cold.

Lucifer strides forward into the fray with Michael at his side. There's no hesitation in their steps. They bear a blade in each hand, and their wings trail behind them, smoke-grey and brilliant white.

This is what angels are. Humanity made us into cherubs, harmless creatures plucking harps on fluffy white clouds, but even weakest of us could make the Earth tremble if pushed.

Righteous fury swirls around Lucifer like a cloak. Once, every demon would have shrunk back at the sight of him, cowering like wolves from a fire. Now they bare their teeth and stand their ground, fear-induced deference forgotten.

The demons' lack of fear doesn't make Lucifer falter for an instant, or if it does, he hides it well. He advances with Michael a step behind. The blackened Hell-forged metal of his blade slices through the throat of the closest demon, nearly cleaving its head off.

That's all it takes.

The rift forgotten, the demons surge forward as one

entity, teeth and claws and the brute strength of numbers pushing forward with the force of the tide.

Grace loses her weapons quickly in the crush, but she isn't an untested innocent anymore. She presses an open palm against the chest of a demon, her lip curling in disgust at touching the creature. The demon lets out a shrill wail of pain as her touch scorches its skin from its very bones.

Uriel started this all those years ago. He tore away the first shield of her humanity with her parents' deaths, exposing the Heavenly blood that draws us all closer like moths to her flame. Michael and Lucifer both pushed her closer to her truth, but it wasn't Michael's misguided attack or Lucifer's love that unfurled her power. It wasn't even blood and resurrection on the slick marble floor of The Saint.

She looked into the jaws of Hell without flinching, when even God's most fearsome son averted his eyes.

The demon slumps to the ground as a burned out husk, and I know whatever the outcome today, Grace will still be standing.

The rest of us are another story.

Elissa and Caila push their way through the crush, hacking and slashing in a futile attempt to reach the rift, but for every demon they pass, two more seem to slither out of the opening. Elissa moves like a blur, a curved knife in each hand, but it's not enough. They're surrounded on all sides, and when a clawed hand slashes across her thigh it's only her quick reflexes that prevents the next slash from disemboweling her.

I'm too far away to do anything but watch, penned in a few feet from Lucifer and Michael, stabbing and punching without even seeing my targets, limbs and faces lost in a red haze.

It's too much.

Lucifer and Michael fight as one unit, knives and wings

slashing through the air, cutting down demons in a movement that almost looks like a grisly ballet. If we weren't all in mortal peril, it would be beautiful.

There are too many.

The demons swarm us like insects, and we're dangerously close to being overwhelmed. None of us will be able to hold this pace for much longer.

Lucifer's hand shoots out, grabbing one of the demons by the throat and hauling it off its feet. The creature looks almost fully human, its features forming a face that looks beautiful, if slightly unsettling in its otherworldliness. High cheekbones and smooth perfect features that could have been carved from marble make it the perfect lure for burning a human to death with their own lust.

Incubus, Asmodeus' favorite children.

The incubus' lips twist into a pout as it squirms in Lucifer's grasp, staring languidly at the Devil through half-lidded eyes. The creature isn't concerned about its predicament. Its nostrils flare as it scents the ripe human lust waiting for it beyond this street.

Lucifer's hand tightens around its throat, and the demon turns the bored gaze to him.

"Who?" Lucifer snarls. "Who is it?" The incubus laughs softly, and Lucifer shakes it, tightening his grip until the demon lets out a pained wheeze.

"Who is trying to wrest control from me? I want a name," he demands.

The demon's lips turn upward, the heat-filled smile that led so many to a vicious death. Lucifer doesn't loosen his grip, and the demon's voice is scarcely more than a rattle in its throat.

"We are called Legion, for we are many."

❧ 6 ❧

CAILA

We run.

I barely notice Lucifer with one of the demons in his grasp. A short demon with one misshapen arm manages to duck past my defenses, and I lose precious seconds grappling with it before I manage to jam a blade between its ribs. Red-black blood spills over my hands, and I fight the instinct to recoil from the thick metallic scent. The demon snaps its jaws at me futilely as I shove it back into a gangly demon creeping toward Grace.

I glance behind me and see Lucifer shaking the demon in his hands like a cat toying with a mouse, but whatever information he's demanding in his interrogation disappears in the din of battle.

Beside me, Elissa is a blur of slashing blades, muttering broken Phoenician words under her breath as she tries to weave protections around us all. She falters, her damaged leg threatening to give out under her but she pushes on. She's stretched thin, and we can't get close enough to the rift to even attempt the spell to seal it.

My attention snaps back to the Devil when I hear

Lucifer's roar of anger. He crushes the demon's throat, cracking its spine with the effort of breaking a toothpick before tossing the limp body to the ground.

Not the answer he was wanting then.

Lucifer's head whips around, scanning the alley as he searches for us, his gaze pausing on Grace and Phenex and finally me.

He nods.

I grab Elissa, pulling her toward the entrance of the alley and away from the rift. Her leg threatens again to buckle under her weight, and she sags heavily against me for a moment before pushing herself away.

Elissa staggers before planting her feet and turning her stubborn gaze at the rift. Power crackles in the air, and it's impossible to think of her as anything but a witch right now. She isn't my world-weary best friend or the woman who somehow commanded the loyalty of one archangel and the love of another.

She's a witch, and a few scratches won't stop her.

Elissa narrows her eyes, staring at the gash in the air. She wavers on her feet, and it pulses as she lists side to side.

I wonder which is the charmer and which is the snake.

Elissa says nothing, but I feel the rush of power pour out of her like a sonic boom. When the next demon attempts to push its way into our world, it can't. The rift bulges outward as the creature tries to claw its way out, but it holds. For now.

Elissa's shoulders drop, and I wrap my arm around her waist for a second time, urging her away from the pack. The flood of magic left the demons that already made it through dazed, but that won't last long.

She doesn't protest the retreat this time, and I take to the air, dragging her skyward. The beating of wings cuts through the pounding of my heart behind me as Phenex and Michael follow. A moment later, Lucifer passes us all, Grace's bloody and battered form cradled in his arms.

"THAT SEAL WON'T HOLD for long."

Our living room has turned into a makeshift infirmary. The archangels immediately shrug off their injuries, but even they look ragged and weary.

This was supposed to be easy.

Michael leans heavily against the scarred wood of the desk, his shirt little more than a bloody rag hanging off the mangled mess of his shoulder. Whichever demon caused that wound must have latched its teeth into the meat of his shoulder like a pitbull, ripping and tearing at his flesh before Michael could fling it away. I'm amazed he was able to fly at all. He rolls his shoulder, wincing as the still-damaged muscle protests the movement.

Lucifer is sprawled out on the grey velvet sofa, one arm flung across his face. The bright living room lights illuminate the dozens of slashes through the fabric of his suit and into his skin. The shallow wounds have long since knit themselves back together, but we're all reeling over the sudden awareness that the creatures of Hell have no fear of him.

Hell has a new master now, or potentially even worse, no master at all.

Every cut, healed or not, is a reminder of that.

Grace sits perched on the arm of the sofa, idly running her fingers through Lucifer's dark hair as if reassuring herself that they both survived another battle.

In another late night talk when I sat on our back porch awaiting the moment when the sun burns away the darkness, Elissa told me of everything Grace willingly put herself through to free me from Brielle's clutches.

We sit side by side, staring out into the black void of our unkempt backyard, and Elissa whispers what they did. What she did.

"We didn't have any other choice. It could have killed her, and I made sure she knew that. Her mind could have just shut down." Elissa wraps her arms around her knees but doesn't look at me.

Whatever she's seeing, it isn't the backyard.

"I thought I was destroying them both to get what I wanted." Elissa's voice is small, barely louder than the faint chirping of crickets from the yard next door. She bites her lip, hesitating so long that I almost give up expecting her to continue.

"I knew you wouldn't have wanted me to risk it. Not with her, but I had to." Elissa turns to face me, and just as she keeps quiet about my new habit of leaving every light in the house blazing, I say nothing about the bright sheen of tears over her eyes.

"I couldn't lose anyone else."

Despite my silent musings, the Last doesn't look up. With the threat gone, at least momentarily, the rest of us have faded into background noise. She and the Devil see nothing but each other.

Serafine's granddaughter has had every ugly truth of Lucifer's past flung into her face. She saw every torment through his eyes and felt every agony written on his skin. Millennia upon millennia of the worst Hell could bring poured into her soul in minutes, and yet she survived.

Even more, she still loves him.

She saw the full extent of his darkness, but to Grace, Lucifer is still the one who lit the stars.

It almost hurts to look at the two of them, scorching my eyes like the brilliant light of the sunset that first day outside of Hell.

I look at her and see echoes of her grandmother and her mother. Serafine and Marianne each had one foot in our world, but they were still so very human. But not Grace. Not anymore.

Even in the chaotic haze of battle, I caught a glimpse of her burning a demon to cinders with just her touch. The others were wise enough to keep their distance after that display, but that illusion of safety wasn't what Grace wanted. The diminutive blonde threw herself into the fray, letting her touch be her weapon, and the monsters built of human nightmares and sins shrunk back from her divine touch.

Not a drop of the blood splattered across her skin belongs to her.

Grace is unharmed. But no one, not even the lover of the Devil himself, can look into the gaping maw of Hell without it changing them. She saw it all through Lucifer's eyes, and now she's seen it with her own.

I'd like to pray that she never gets closer to Hell than this, but I don't know who would hear my prayers anymore.

Elissa took the most damage of all of us. I stayed glued to her back, cutting through the horde and letting the worst brunt of injuries fall to me, but it wasn't enough. I called up the long-forgotten memories of battle as I tested the weight of a blade in my hand, and just as I did millennia ago, I felt like a pretender.

I have never been a warrior, but in the celestial wars I put aside my wishes and duties and fought against the Fallen, all the while trying to forget that I had once called them brothers and sisters.

We did as we were told, shutting off the parts of ourselves that screamed in agony at harming one of our own. The light went out in Michael's eyes, but he wasn't alone in his darkness.

Heaven changed that day, and it wasn't just due to the Lightbringer's absence. But those that survived adapted and tried to forget the names of those that fell. Like amputees, we learned to walk again, but the phantom pains never stopped.

I did everything within my power to shield her, but Elissa

still caught three deep gashes across her thigh, dangerously close to tearing open her the femoral artery and spilling her life's blood in a dirty alleyway. Lucifer's gift means she heals far faster than a human, but the demonic claws nearly cleaved her leg open to the bone. Elissa didn't help matters with draining her dwindling reserves to slap a temporary seal on the rift. She'll be laid up for at least a few days.

I douse the cuts with holy water, and Elissa hisses in surprised pain as demonic essence bubbles up like an infection. I've barely finished bandaging her leg before she's yanking her ruined jeans back up and hobbling outside to check the wards with Michael rushing after her.

Phenex stands by the front door, his eyes darting to stare through the security gate every few moments. He's checking that the legions of Hell didn't follow our trail right to the doorstep.

It's foolish, but I understand.

His face is carefully blank, his eyes focused on nothing but the threatening world outside our front steps. Phenex clenches and unclenches his hands as his split knuckles heal, and I don't miss the tremors going through them.

I'm quickly losing the fight to keep my own hands still now that there are no wounds left to bandage and nothing else to fix.

This was all too much, too soon.

"We had to leave," Phenex counters without looking away from the window.

Lucifer sits up, every muscle looking as though he's tensing for another fight, but he looks around the room and sees the state we're all in. Wounded. Shell-shocked. If we had stayed, we might have won, but we also might have died.

Lucifer closes his eyes and sighs, "We'll be prepared next time."

"How?" It's Grace that speaks up. She hasn't moved, and

Lucifer opens his mouth to reply before snapping it shut a moment later, the last remnants of fight draining from him. "We know the location of one rift. One. We don't know where the others are or even how many Brielle made." Grace cuts her eyes over to Phenex, and none of us need to read her soul to know that she's remembering the shattered creature who hid in her spare room like a ghost.

"There could be two more rifts, or there could be twenty." Grace falls silent for a moment, pinching the bridge of her nose before fixing Lucifer with a desperate look. "Uriel almost killed you, and this. . . this feels so much worse." Her voice breaks on her last word, just the tiniest fissure but Lucifer hears it.

She's afraid.

We all are.

Somewhere in the house, Michael is trying to convince Elissa to sit down long enough to allow her body to heal, remembering years without her.

Lucifer twists a coil of Grace's hair around his finger, ignoring the dried blood trapped in her curls.

And I watch Phenex as he stares out the window, counting moments in the tick of his clenched jaw as he tries to stay still and silent.

For the first time, we all have something to lose.

I hardly notice Lucifer and Grace as they leave. They slip past Phenex, a united front against whatever might be lurking in the dark, and when the security gate clangs shut behind them, Phenex and I are left alone.

I want. . . I don't know what I want. I want to close my eyes without the fear that I'll open them to blinding darkness. I want to wash away the taste of damp stone and blood from my mouth that never seems to fade.

I turn my back on Phenex before I do something we'll both regret. I grab the abandoned rocks glasses scattered around the living room, watery dregs of whiskey swirling with the last few slivers of ice. If there was ever a night for the hard stuff, it's tonight.

I disappear into the kitchen, keeping my back to Phenex with the illusion of separation, but the open floor plan of the house doesn't give me any place to hide.

I dump the remnants of the liquor down the sink, the smoky scent of whiskey rising up from the drain. I feel off balance, like the room's too bright and too warm. I wear Elissa's borrowed clothes, my usual attire not being exactly suitable for a war, and the faded grey jeans and black tank top feel wrong on my body, like every drop of color has been bled out of me.

"Caila."

His voice is quiet. Barely more than a whisper in the still room. We both grew accustomed to the silence and the darkness. The world outside still feels too loud, too bright. Ever since Brielle ripped us apart I've felt adrift, a leaf caught in a storm drain. Everything swirls around me and I can't seem to figure out which way is up.

I don't turn around. I feel his eyes on my back, and it's hard not to marvel at that. He can see me. If I was brave enough to turn around, I could see him too.

"Caila." His voice is closer. He hovers a few steps behind me, close but still not close enough.

I want. . .

I should turn around before I can lose my nerve. The flat soles of my shoes squeak on the floor as I hesitate. Another thing borrowed from Elissa. Another shield to wrap myself in. I feel like a burn victim, like everything protecting me has been scorched away leaving me as just one raw nerve.

And the only one who can possibly understand is standing right behind me, staring at my back with his sky blue eyes.

The first time we kissed was in Hell. We fumbled through

the darkness to find each other. Phenex gave me the strength to survive, but I think I'm part of what broke him.

Maybe this can put both of us back together.

"Caila." I feel his breath against the back of my neck, and my fingers curl around the lip of the sink as my body turns to liquid.

I'm an angel. I never fell. I never defected. But still, somehow I ended up condemned. The second Fallen is pressed against my back, and for the first time since Brielle's chain snapped around my neck I feel like I can breathe.

I turn around.

I'm not sure which of us sought the other in the darkness. Maybe we both just wanted that brief respite from our torments. Maybe I'm foolish for thinking that it's more than that. Maybe I should let the past lie.

Instead, I stand up on my toes inside a pair of borrowed sneakers and press my lips against his.

Phenex's lips stay closed. I feel the shudder that runs through his body, and I know he's remembering.

I keep my eyes open.

The kitchen lights are too bright, their harsh glow illuminating two broken souls in ripped and bloody clothing clinging to each other in a messy kitchen.

Once, I chided Elissa for every misplaced glass and unwashed plate. I miss being the person who fretted over such trivialities.

Now, I lose focus of everything but the pale gold of Phenex's eyelashes against the dark shadows under his eyes.

I feel the dam break in him when he starts to kiss me back, and I swallow the urge to sob. My hands are still clenched around the edge of the counter, and I can hardly keep myself upright.

I think of Elissa, think of Grace, and I wonder. *Is this what they feel?* Is this what made Grace wade through the mire of Lucifer's soul and what led Elissa to finally forgive?

I let go of the counter, and I lace one of my hands through his, feeling the tendons flex and move and remembering torn nails and broken fingers.

Phenex pulls back just a hair's breadth, and his eyes open. His pupils are blown wide, black swallowing up the blue, and he looks lighter. He looks whole.

I wonder if I look the same.

Then the shutters fall, and he takes a quick step backward. His hand falls from mine, and I already miss the contact.

"This can't happen," he says. His gaze darts around the room, flitting from the darkened hallway that leads to the bedrooms to the front door to the black square of the tiny kitchen window behind me.

Anywhere but me.

"This can't. . ." he trails off, scrubbing his hand across his face. "*We* can't. . ." He takes another step back from me like I'm something he needs to run from.

I suppose I am.

I turn back to the sink so I don't have to watch him walk away, but I still jump when the front door slams behind him.

7

PHENEX

I still feel her lips against mine, the sensation carved into my skin deeper than the scar bisecting my throat.

Any port in a storm. That's the lie I told myself as we clung to each other in the darkness.

She could have been anyone. Fallen. Angel. Human. My desperate, broken psyche would have grown devoted to anyone. She was nothing special.

I was nothing special.

But I remember her singing to me.

She doesn't know what she's doing. She can't, or else she'd run from me, from this house, from everything this broken city represents. If she had any sense of self-preservation, she'd spread those golden wings and let them carry her back up to Heaven and away from us all.

Grace's fate was sealed long before her birth, Elissa's the moment Michael crossed her doorstep. They chose their archangels and the messy chaos of this world over the gates of Heaven, but neither of them has been to Hell. They made their choices out of righteous anger and unlikely love, but they don't truly know what they chose.

Grace walked in the halls of Lucifer's mind for a spell, but it's not the same as walking among the tattered souls and watching as they're broken down a bit more each day.

How many more centuries of torment under Brielle's manicured fingers would it have taken to twist me into a demon? If she'd had her way, would I be slithering out of a rift beside them, ready to exact my own pound of flesh from the ripe fruit of this world?

They don't know what Hell is.

I do. And so does Caila.

She'll never be the same. There's nothing I can do about that now. The angel who stumbled into my prison in broken high heels and a dress fit for a debutante is dead, but if she returns to Heaven she might be able to move forward. She might be able to heal.

I won't drag her down with me.

I look up and see the flickering spark of an aging streetlight casting the road in a jaundiced glow as my mind tries to untwist from the tangle I've trapped myself in.

The scent of lush flowers on her skin, Eden bottled for mass consumption.

The soft sigh in her throat when my hand brushed her hip and the creak of the countertop as she leaned against it.

The promise of comfort, and maybe, just maybe something more, followed by the icy reminder of just what happened to both of us the last time I allowed myself to touch her.

The security gate slamming like a gunshot in my wake as I ran away.

I wander the unfamiliar streets, the houses a darkened blur, the heavy scent of rot from the Mississippi riding the breeze. I don't care where my feet are taking me, but my steps aren't fast enough to outpace my thoughts.

I stretch out my wings. They're stiff from long disuse, and

the feathers still look the worse for wear, but they're whole. The short escape flight today was the first time I flew since. . . before, and I want to taste the wind again.

I need to remind myself that I'm free.

I take to the air, flying up and up and up. Below me, the city lights recede to faint golden pinpricks as the air grows thin and cool. The wind rushes past my ears, blocking out the endless din inside my head with pure blank nothingness.

Funny how now I long for silence.

I wheel through the air, spiraling through clouds, twisting and turning until I forget which way is up and my wings ache and I can finally *breathe*.

The bright lights of the Superdome glow like a sunrise in the distance when I make my descent, and I realize where I am just before my feet touch the ground.

I land outside the wrought-iron gate, the blackened metal still standing sentry around the burned-out ruin in front of me.

The mansion.

Echoes of magic still cling to the grounds like reverb from an amplifier long after the last note has played. The gate hangs crookedly, one broken hinge still valiantly holding it upright, and it groans like a dying bird when I push it open.

The fire has long since been extinguished, but the scent of char fills my nose. The grass crunches under my feet, burned to a cinder that even the most well-paid gardeners would be hard pressed to revive.

I move like a dream, following the line of the iron fence and skirting around the debris that litters the yard, burnt siding and hunks of wood blackened into charcoal. The piles of rubble grow larger the closer I get to the ruin of the house. I hear the tinkle of crystal as my foot brushes the remnants of a chandelier, the sparkling monstrosity that hung in the entryway reduced to a pile of dull grey shards.

Heaven caused this. That's what Lucifer told me, sneering as he spoke her name. *She dared to love a Nephilim, and we all know what happens to them. Heaven twisted her love into something vile.*

It wouldn't be the first time.

Brielle. Her name means hunting grounds, and she made sport of us all. Heaven wronged her, and she chose to set the world alight to warm her hands on the blaze.

I hate her, but I can't blame her for that. Heaven stole her life, so she stole another.

There are no answers here. Lucifer was right. If Brielle ever opened a portal here, she sealed it tight long before Lucifer and Michael immolated her palace. There are no demons crawling through the rubble, and Hell does not whisper to me.

At least, not any louder than it does anywhere else in the wide world.

I close my eyes, and I still feel the collar around my neck. I still see flashes of auburn hair and pale silk and a smile like a knife. She liked the finer things. In another life, we might have enjoyed them together or at least whiled away a few pleasurable hours in our respective eternities.

I almost laugh at that. What happened to the Phenex who slaked his thirst for life in whatever pretty creature caught his fancy? Once I ticked off my favorite sins, passing time in lust and gluttony while my old friend pride whispered honeyed words in my ears.

Wine, women, and song. An old saying, though not nearly as old as me, and for the first time, I'm beginning to feel it.

Unwanted in Heaven, and barred from Hell. Lucifer told me to make the wide world my own, but I can't seem to take a step forward without ending up back here. We're all a tangled mess, the strands of our lives snarled together across the centuries, and I understand Lucifer's perpetual rage at our Father far better than I ever did before.

I chose to fall on Lucifer's words, but for the first time in years beyond remembering I *understand*.

Everything we do seems to just be another test that we're set up to fail.

Lucifer fell, and I followed a step behind him. The loss of his brother broke Michael enough to let a witch, a *human* into his heart, but he was still Heaven's slave. Just as he broke Lucifer's bones on the rocks, he shattered his witch so completely that her torment echoed through Hell.

And Lucifer, still boiling in his own hatred, came calling.

Elissa wandered across the centuries to find the Nephilim and *his* witch. I don't need to wonder if she saw herself and Michael in that pair. She wears grief and guilt across her like a shroud, and she flinches every time she looks at me. They were poor substitutes for Michael, but some part of her loved them, and she hates herself for that.

Something of Heaven crawled under Elissa's skin, and for the third time, she let herself be taken with another angel. Pretty and fair with a voice like a bell, Caila was what Heaven once was, and what we all long to be in the depths of our hearts.

I wish I'd known her before. I would like to have seen the unspoiled goodness in her eyes.

She was what we *wished* Heaven once was.

And then there is the Last. An angel, a witch, even a loa followed her bloodline, hovering around the lives of her mother, her grandmother, even further back. We all watched from a distance until the summer day when a tiny blonde with sad eyes brushed against Lucifer in the square and threw this all into motion.

It's hard to feel like anything but a puppet on a string, dancing for His divine amusement.

"Phenex."

I tense at his voice, and I hate myself for the reaction.

Even after I tried to sell his great love to Michael for a second chance, even when the word *Judas* danced on his tongue and he looked at me with such betrayal, I never feared him.

Now I shrink from the sound of his voice like a penitent awaiting the scourge. Yet another comfort stolen from me.

I feel my lips curve upward into what I hope is some bland approximation of a smile before I turn around.

By this point in my existence, I should know that you can't fool the Devil.

"I thought this place deserved another look." I gesture lamely at the house, my explanation failing to convince either of us. Lucifer doesn't spare a glance at the remnants of the house scattered around us as he strides through the broken gate to where I stand. His coal-black eyes stay laser-focused on me.

"Where's Grace?" I ask, grasping at another deflection. It doesn't work either, though I see the faintest flicker in his eyes at her name.

Shattered glass and spilled liquor decorates the floor of The Saint, and my chest still aches from the first gasping breath after she laid her hands on me, knitting together torn skin with her touch.

She smiled at me when I handed her the bottle. No hesitation. No expectations. Only the knowledge that I meant something to Lucifer, and for her, that was enough. The three of us sipped room-temperature vodka, sitting in the quiet aftermath of Uriel's rage.

And I felt alive.

Resurrected.

Free.

A few days later, I'd be in chains, but in that moment, she healed me, and Lucifer forgave me. In that moment, we forgave each other, and I could forget Heaven and Hell.

In that moment, surrounded by the rubble of a hotel bar, I felt more peace that I had in centuries.

Lucifer's head cocks to the side as he watches me. They

all think I don't notice the way their eyes follow me, tracking every movement, every tiny tremor, every flinch. I know he's still expecting me to crumble to pieces and slip back into catatonia any moment.

He's not wrong.

"Where did you go?" Lucifer asks, taking a step closer. My conscious mind knows that this is the real Lucifer, still wearing the same ripped suit, sartorial obsessions forgotten in the face of the real concern buried in his gaze.

Nonetheless, I recoil from him, my back striking the fence with enough force to make the metal groan.

Lucifer stills, and I watch as his mind connects the dots in my behavior. He knows Hell's greatest torments, after all. He was the architect of most of them.

"There's something you left out, isn't there?"

I nod stiffly, waiting for him to continue his train of thought aloud.

Tell the truth and shame the Devil.

He says nothing.

Why doesn't he come?

He takes a step backward, and I'm not strong enough to hide the sudden lessening of tension, my muscles relaxing in increments with each scrap of distance between us. Lucifer's head dips, his eyes concentrating on the web of cracks in the pavement below our feet.

Still, he says nothing. I watch as he nods ever so slightly as if bracing himself to ask the question hanging in the air.

"Was it me?"

I don't answer at first. Giving voice to it makes it real, makes it so much harder to bury beneath a thousand other regrets.

I want to lie. I want to shake my head and paste a false smile across my lips. It would be so much easier to seal every memory away, entomb every cut and burn and scream so deep within me that I can forget.

But if tonight has taught us anything at all, it's taught us that nothing stays buried for long. One day, every sick memory will slither its way to the forefront of my mind.

You can't hide in there forever.

It wasn't him, not really. I'm not so broken that I don't realize that. The hands that mangled my wings weren't really Lucifer's, but it was still his face that I stared up at from the cold ground. It was still his voice laughing as I choked on my own blood.

I know it wasn't him that left me wrecked and ruined in the darkness, but my lips still form the answer to his question.

"Yes."

Lucifer doesn't react at first. His jaw tightens, and his eyelids fall shut as though some deep part of him is crumpling inward at my admission. Before my eyes, he seems to age a thousand years before snapping back into control and opening his eyes.

"I'm sorry," he says, and I hear every apology hidden beneath those two words.

I'm sorry for everything that bitch did to you.

I'm sorry she wore my face and my voice.

I'm sorry for Uriel's blade and for Michael's lie.

Most of all, I'm sorry I dragged you into my rebellion in the first place.

"It wasn't you," I reply, and Lucifer forces his lips into a weak smile.

Once, he was everything to me. My only true friend, and the one who showed me the door out of Heaven's gilded cage.

Will he ever look at me with anything but pity again?

"That doesn't really matter, does it Phenex?" Lucifer looks past my shoulder, staring at the burned-out husk of the mansion behind me, and the loathing in his eyes could set it alight again. "I wish Michael had left her alive."

The humans like to imagine the Devil as the torturer standing above each damned soul, a stash of implements of pain laid out beside him like a surgeon's tools. Never mind the sheer logistics of doling out pain to every soul languishing in Hell; like a Santa Claus of suffering, somehow Lucifer would find time for every sinner.

Long ago, he tried to do just that. The cruelest souls, those vile, blackened hearts that reveled in the pain of others, drinking down the tears of their fellow man like sweet wine. . . those caught his attention.

They were the ones that proved him right, after all.

Flawed. Vicious. Evil.

We were meant to worship *them*? Love *them* above all else?

He would gaze upon the worst humanity had to offer. He would look it in the face and memorize it.

And then he would pick up a knife.

Brielle will never know how fortunate she is to have met her death after Lucifer defected from Hell.

He lifts his hand as if to reach for my shoulder before faltering and dropping it to his side.

"Don't hesitate to seize whatever happiness you can, Phenex," he murmurs. I don't need to ask what he means. Or who. They all watch me, waiting for the inevitable meltdown when poor, broken Phenex crumbles to ashes, but only Caila stays close enough to touch. Only Caila slips past the defenses that have me flinching away from every loud noise.

Only Caila's voice singing snatches of old standards on the floor of Grace's spare room led me through the darkness and back into the bright light of the real world.

Of course, Lucifer noticed.

He takes another step backward, his mouth a tight line as

I relax just a bit more at the distance. He nods, his face unreadable, and I turn away from him.

"We've all lost too much time on the past," he adds, the soft sound of wing beats following as he takes flight.

I'm left alone beside the ruin, staring at charred plaster and broken wood as if I could read my future in the wreckage like tea leaves.

8

CAILA

He avoids me.

We're all on edge. Constant awareness of just how temporary Elissa's fix might be prickles against our senses, robbing us of anything but the most fleeting moments of rest.

Hell's bleeding into this world, bringing the nightmare I thought I escaped to my door, and we might not be able to stop them this time. No one wants to admit that out loud, but it's written in Lucifer's sharp words and Michael's quiet intensity as he sharpens his blades.

Hell is coming, and I feel like I might be able to endure it with Phenex by my side. I almost have to laugh at how far I've fallen from who I once was.

Lucifer and Michael patrol the city, armed to the teeth and ready to dispatch any demon they find back to Hell. Night after night they return to our doorstep weary and spattered with blackened blood, but the growing number of demon corpses is far from comforting.

Demons aren't pack animals. Trust doesn't come naturally to a creature wrought of evil and corruption, so the demonic horde scattered to the winds as soon as they wriggled free from the rift.

The two archangels have spent the last week picking off lone demons foolish enough to draw attention to themselves. They catch the stupid ones, the soldier demons that thrive on chaos and use nothing beyond brute strength and fear to achieve it. Every encounter has barely been a fight, but Lucifer's nerves are still coiled like a spring. He stays on high alert, snapping at Michael whenever the tension ratchets up another notch because he knows they weren't all that escaped.

I know the list running through his head. We've all heard the names muttered under his breath as he paces.

Asmodeus. Abaddon. Malphas. Azazel. Belial. Astaroth.

It could be any of them. It could be *all* of them. Hell's most wicked Fallen, the ones who chose to make the fields of the damned their own personal playground.

None of us want to think about the havoc they'll cause in this world.

When both archangels walk through the front door for the second night in a row with swords still gleaming and unmarred by demon blood, it's Michael who gives a voice to our worries.

"They've obscured themselves from us," he says, dropping wearily onto the overstuffed armchair.

A quiet night should be reason to celebrate, but one glance at Lucifer tells me all I need to know. There's no way their body count matches up with what escaped the rift, and the lower level demons aren't smart enough to lay low without someone much more powerful giving them that order.

Better mayhem in the streets than this fabricated calm.

At Michael's words, Elissa barely looks up from the worn spell book she pours over. While the archangels scour the city, my best friend drowns herself in faded parchment in a frantic attempt to find the remaining rifts and permanently seal them.

She disappears into the city without mentioning her destination, and her silence stings. Elissa's independence has always been at the forefront of her personality, but once we were a team. Now the bike engine revs, and she's gone, only to return a few hours later with even more thick tomes bulging out of her bike's saddlebags. The pungent scent of herbs and the sweet smoke of incense from Erzulie's shop clings to her clothes and hair. She barely spares me a glance before she's rifling through the books.

I've begged her not to blame herself for Brielle's crimes.

She saved me, risking life and limb and sanity to rip through Brielle's defenses, but in the dark corners of her mind, it wasn't enough, and now she forgets all else but this new obsession with balancing the scales.

Michael pries the book from her fingers, shaking his head in silence when she protests. And for once, she relents. I catch her eye as she stumbles to her bedroom to snatch a few well needed hours of sleep before the cycle repeats itself tomorrow. Elissa pulls the corners of her lips upward in a weak smile that doesn't reach her eyes.

Fatigue has weakened her internal defenses enough that the shrouds she wraps her soul in are paper thin, and I let my senses brush against her. It's a betrayal that I never allowed myself to indulge in before, not once in decades of friendship.

Even in the safety of her home, she's still guarded, and all I hear are whispers.

You brought this on them.

You brought this on her.

Broken. Ruined. Damaged.

I pull back before Elissa realizes what I'm doing. She

squeezes my shoulder as she passes me with Michael at her heels.

"Talk tomorrow?" she asks, a tentative note to her voice that I've never heard.

"Of course," I reply automatically. Underneath, I'm still reeling at the brief glimpse.

Broken. Ruined. Damaged.

That's what she sees me as now. That's what they all see me as.

Grace watches from the other armchair. Her bare feet are curled under the hem of her skirt. She still cloaks herself in the same uniform of sundresses and ballet flats she's worn since returning to New Orleans, and however foolish it might be, it makes me miss my own clothes. I miss bright colors and patterns, the click of heels on the floorboards, the swish of fabric around my knees when I move. The world is burning around us, and I wish I was brave enough to meet the flames in my own clothing.

Yet every time I reach into my wardrobe, brushing my hands through the tangle of color bursting through the doors all I see is that sky blue dress I wore when she took me. All I hear is the crack of my heel breaking as I fought, that snap making me falter just enough for Brielle to win.

I shut the wardrobe door, wishing I could shut out the memories just as easily. And I reach for another borrowed pair of black jeans.

Unaware of my inner turmoil, Grace pages idly through one of the few spell books Elissa has that's written in English. She doesn't expect to find anything worthwhile on the pages, but she's just as desperate as I am to feel useful.

She closes the book none too gently, a faint puff of dust escaping the pages. Grace sighs, glaring at the faded brown leather of the cover as though personally offended that it didn't contain the answers she needed.

"I feel like we're just spinning our wheels," she says, dropping the book onto the coffee table beside the growing stack that Elissa has already discarded as useless. "Are we really just going to have to sit back and wait for the city to explode to stop this?"

Lucifer stands by the front door, staring out into the night. His voice is clipped, his shoulders stiff and wary as he scrutinizes the shadows beneath the burned-out streetlights for movement. Just like that first night, nothing has followed us. The legions of Hell aren't clawing at our door.

Yet.

He doesn't look away from the window when he speaks. "If I thought you'd listen, I'd tell you to leave the city until I handle this." Grace barely manages to inhale, a protest already on her lips before Lucifer glances back at her with a wry smile. "I know you won't leave," he adds, putting the argument to rest before it beings. "And if I lock you up, you'll just bust the door down."

Grace unfolds herself from the chair, padding to Lucifer's side on bare feet, her shoes abandoned by the sofa. Some part of me still wants to warn her away from him. Habits built on millennia of parroting the idea that Lucifer is the ultimate evil are hard to break.

The Last made her choice, driving a blade through Uriel's throat for love of the Devil. And she does love him. Even more shocking, he returns her devotion, and I'm beginning to realize just how far the distance is between Heaven's proclamations and the actual truth.

Grace presses herself against the length of Lucifer's body, murmuring, "There's not a door strong enough to keep me away." The Devil chuckles at her words before kissing her, my presence forgotten.

There's a story there, one that I missed in the madness Uriel unleashed on the city just a few short weeks ago. Under the playfulness of her voice, there's an edge to her words, a sharp tone reminding him that Grace isn't the little woman that needs his protection.

Feeling like an intruder, I flip open another of Elissa's books, staring at the page without seeing the words as anything but a black and white jumble.

"There's nothing we can do but what we're already doing," Lucifer says, finally giving up on his vigil by the front door. "We don't exactly have a long list of allies."

I glance up from my unread page and meet Lucifer's dark stare. I know just whose name is hovering at the forefront of his mind.

Phenex. I haven't seen him since our ill-fated kiss, and his absence from our little group is jarring. Every night, Lucifer and Michael return from their hunt. They check if Elissa has made any lucky breakthroughs in her research and debrief us on the night's incidents. Phenex is never with them.

No one speaks of Phenex's conspicuous absence, but I'm not blind to the curious looks Elissa and Grace cast my way.

The Devil and his beloved leave, slipping out the front door into the waiting darkness, returning to the nicer side of town where the grass hasn't all withered in the heat and the windows don't have bars.

And cloistered away in Grace's childhood bedroom like a dark secret is Phenex.

I wonder, is he my dark secret? Am I his?

Lucifer's words dig at my brain. *We don't exactly have a long list of allies.*

He's right. Word of Michael siding with Lucifer in the recent battles would have certainly reached Heaven by now. Michael's position might be high enough that he could escape consequences for a lot of transgressions, but not this.

Heaven is many things, but forgiving is rarely one. Once word of Michael allying himself with the Fallen One reaches the other angels, his status as an archangel won't be enough to protect him.

But what of me? I haven't fallen. Brielle did not pry the secrets of Heaven from my lips.

What is that old saying? The enemy of my enemy is my friend.

No matter how little they care for humanity, no angel would be willing to sit by and allow Hell to win. Even if their aid is only fueled by competitive spite, that's enough.

I know what I need to do.

I need to go home.

IT'S BEEN decades since the last time my feet touched the ground within Heaven, but even blind I would know the way.

I'm not confident enough to stroll in through the gates and announce my presence, nor am I foolhardy enough to beg for an audience with Metatron, though his aid is what we truly need. Our Father's voice has never been quiet about his dislike for the other archangels, Michael especially. Envy is an ugly word, but it's fitting.

I am not so naïve as to think my time with Elissa has gone unnoticed. Heaven was never my enemy, but has my absence made me the enemy of Heaven?

I slip into my home like a thief, searching for any familiar faces from my old garrison and finding none. It's unsurprising that after Uriel's descent into madness we scattered. His failings were our own.

And just how many agreed with his actions?

It's not a question I need to ask when I already know the answer.

Far too many.

When I last walked these paths, I was innocent. I'd

lived thousands of years, watched wars and bloodshed in Heaven and on Earth and seen it for the foolishness it always is. I'd seen the humans grow from creatures scratching a living out of dust and stone to beings that could harness the power of the elements, making their cities shine as bright as Heaven. I'd lived so long, but I still blindly believed the words of all those who called themselves my betters.

I've heard it said that a frog will leap to freedom if you toss it into a pot of boiling water, but if the temperature rises bit by bit it will sit calmly as it boils to death.

Uriel did not go from the placid guardian of Eden to a raving madman in a day, but bit by bit his sanity slipped away from him, falling like dying petals ground under his feet in the Garden. Lucifer fell. Father abandoned us to our own devices, and Uriel walked into the Garden and never really left again.

Angels are not made to be solitary. The voices of our brothers and sisters echo around us always, and the low hum of prayers fill up the background noise.

There is no true silence in Heaven, but the Garden dampens the noise, swallowing the voices in lush blooms and rich soil. And in that silence, Uriel planned his attacks.

Rose was barely cold in her grave, and Serafine little more than a teenager, her hatred at her father's cruelties so close to the boiling point when I made my decision. There was no overheard clandestine meeting, no stroll through Eden where Uriel issued her death warrant, but it was always understood. Serafine would be next, and if luck was on Heaven's side the polluted bloodline would end with her.

Serafine would die, but I never understood *why*.

Death had followed Uriel through the centuries. The fire that swept through the Quarter that consumed Arelia decades before was his doing. Genevieve drowned herself in the depths of the Mississippi rather than give him the satisfaction of killing her with his own hands.

After Genevieve, Uriel learned subtlety. Wards surrounded Rose, thick as briars, making her invisible and untouchable to not just him but all angels. Erzulie had a hand in that, her fingers following the bloodline as far back as Uriel ever did. But the souls of some men are weak, and it takes only the lightest touch to push them down the path to corruption.

I never found out who Uriel sent on that errand, but the outcome was the same. One of my brothers or sisters slipped into Sacriste's confidence, whispering treachery in his ears.

"Your wife speaks madness. Lock her away."

The souls of men are weak, and Rose's trusting heart suffered for it. The walls of the asylum shouldn't have been enough to keep her from Uriel's grasp, especially not for the years she languished there. She should have grown weaker, the tangle of wards falling away from her like dying vines. Erzulie had a hand in that as well, but the loa never trusted me enough to share that information.

Not that I blame her.

When Rose's body smashed on the cobblestones that September night, I stopped being able to watch from the sidelines.

I didn't stay behind to reason with those that had already been lost to Uriel's thrall. I didn't curse their choices and make one desperate stand for righteousness.

I simply slipped away and did not return.

We are not prisoners in Heaven. Any angel can come and go as we please, and I have never been important enough to warrant a true summons. If I was honest with myself, my absence likely wasn't noticed for years.

I hid in the shadows. I watched Serafine grow fearless, bucking against her father's suspicious yoke until the day he pushed her too far, and the Quarter glowed with flames again.

"Those old houses, you know. The whole place went up."

I followed her to the edge of the country, to the bright turquoise of the Pacific ocean and the gleam of the Hollywood sign, but Serafine was no trusting fool.

"Why are you following me?" she snarled, shoving me against the pristine whitewashed storefront. The streets were crowded as locals and tourists alike came to worship at the glorious edifice to consumerism. A pair of housewives with flawlessly lacquered red lips and hair teased and set within an inch of its life paused to gawk at us. Serafine took a step backward, glaring daggers at me.

"Talk," she hissed, no fear in her voice.

I did.

THE ENTRANCE to the Garden still sits empty. No other angel seems ready to take up Uriel's posting, and I can't keep from wondering what rumors my brothers and sisters are taking as truth now. Have Uriel's crimes turned him into a villain equal to Lucifer or has his death made him a martyr?

I duck into the Garden, the thick nectar of the air wrapping around me, and I find this place working it's magic on me, relaxing my tense nerves. With the wild, untamed splendor of Eden surrounding me, it's easy to let the scent of a thousand blooms lull my senses.

This is my home, after all.

My eyes fall shut, and a tiny, traitorous thought creeps into my mind.

I could stay.

In truth, I don't think any of them would blame me. Grace has Lucifer to protect her now, and he's far more formidable than I could ever hope to be against the forces of Heaven or Hell.

Elissa has her Michael again. Her heart is finally whole after so many years of solitude and regret. She doesn't need me anymore.

None of them need me anymore.

And here, I could have peace.

I walk aimlessly, my feet taking me down a random path cutting through the greenery. Fallen leaves and sticks crunch with each of my steps. The path twists and turns, leading me deeper into the endless depths of Eden. To my left, wide swaths of purple heather begin to give way to heavier vegetation. The trees grow closer, their thick trunks nearly touching at some points. The sharp scent of fallen needles and the bitter tannic odor of the oak leaves grows, blocking out the softer floral perfumes.

Eden is not just a manicured flower garden. All of the plants of the Earth ramble across its grounds, from the tiniest lichen clinging to a rock to the redwoods that scrape the skies.

The way grows darker as the path winds through the trees like a serpent. Few bother exploring Eden beyond the easy trails through the pretty flowers. The branches brush against my arms, bony fingers of trees that were ancient when the Earth was young.

I could stay.

I stop.

Silence surrounds me, the hum of Heaven muffled by the trees and the soil. Heaven has no wind, no rain, no seasons, yet the trees creak and the leaves rustle around me.

I see how Uriel let himself grow lost here.

There have always been whispers through the garrison that no angel has ever reached the end of Eden. One can follow the paths for miles or take to the air and fly until their wings falter, but it never ends.

Perhaps it's where our Father retreated to when he left us alone.

Or maybe Uriel finally reached the end and what he found there drove him mad.

I sink to the ground, leaning against an oak tree, the trunk nearly as wide as a car. I stretch my legs out before me, and a few fallen leaves cling to the faded denim of my borrowed jeans. I tilt my head back, staring up at the canopy so many feet above. The leaves are dense, only a few golden beams of light filtering down to me, but I still cherish the warmth on my face.

I wonder if he remembers this place?

The thought slips into my mind as unexpectedly as he slipped into my heart.

I could stay.

I want to stay.

"Phenex."

It's barely a whisper, but his is a name that hasn't been spoken in Heaven for so long. The Second Fallen. Lucifer's right hand. The one who held me in the darkness.

He chose to leave this all behind. We have that in common. He chose Hell, chose Lucifer, and freedom at whatever the cost.

What did I chose? A cause I lost over and over again. Serafine. Marianne. Even Grace. The Last didn't need me to save her skin. She brought the Devil to his knees and put an archangel in his grave.

The wide world is still out there, but as I breathe in the warm air of Eden, it's easy to forget.

But not him.

Not Phenex.

I love him too much.

The thought hits me with a jolt, and I open my eyes to stare at the shafts of light peaking through the leaves.

It was in darkness we met. It was in fear that we forgot our pasts and our histories, forgot Fallen and angel, forgot anything but breath and touch and the whisper of each other's voices in the blackness.

I look around at the thick screen of trees surrounding me and the thin ribbon of the path snaking between them, beckoning me deeper.

I would be so easy to stay, to cloister myself away among the flowers and the trees and forget the memory of rough iron and cold stone.

But he would be alone.

My fingers sink into the soft soil at the base of the tree as I push myself to my feet. I turn back towards the direction of the gate, walking away without any more hesitation.

I've wasted enough time.

I'M NEARLY to the gate when I realize I'm no longer alone.

An angel stands sentry by a cluster of purple lilacs. I see him in profile, his face hidden from my searching gaze. A light grey suit clothes his lean frame, and deep brown hair falls in soft waves down the back of his neck. From where I stand, he looks harmless, but just as they are in Hell, appearances can be deceiving here.

The instinct to flee surges in me, misplaced adrenaline urging me to back silently down the path and disappear into the trees and the darkness. Darkness took Uriel, twisted him into something vicious and cruel. It warped Phenex into something broken and lost, and me. . . I'm still learning everything the darkness did to me.

I rock back, and I wish for a fallen branch to snap under

my heel or the crunch of dried leaves to alert him. Anything that keeps me from having to choose.

Eden stays silent though, and the Garden seems to hold its breath until the angel tilts his head toward me. The warm glow of the afternoon sun hits his face, revealing the gentle slop of his cheekbones and wide eyes the color of amber, darting around the Garden and surveying all he sees.

It takes too long for my sluggish brain to recognize him, but once his name springs into my mind I can't stop myself from calling out to him.

"Sariel!"

To say that Sariel looks shocked to see me is an understatement so deep it's almost laughable. His head whips in the direction of my voice before freezing to stare, blinking his eyes owlishly for a moment as if he's not entirely certain that I'm real and not at a mirage or some specter conjured out of the ether. His brow furrows, his eyes narrowing before he whispers "Caila?"

"It's me," I answer. The sudden adrenaline dump has me twitchy and unbalanced, but this is Sariel, one of the few in my garrison that I have never doubted. I barely realize my feet are moving until I'm scant yards away from him.

For the first time, I'm beginning to realize just how starved for the company of my own kind I've been. Fallen they might be, but Lucifer and Phenex are still of Heaven. They have seen the hidden ugliness of this place, but they've also seen its glory. Even Michael's aloof presence has been like a balm in these past few weeks, soothing me with his proximity and the hum against my senses that reads *home*.

I stop just short of Sariel, barely registering that he hasn't moved from where he stands.

"You've returned?" The question is light, his voice flat and without emotion, the shock that filled it a few moments ago gone as if it never existed.

I take his hands in mine, squeezing them briefly before releasing them. His hands are cool, the skin dry, and I've been on Earth for far too long because my first thought is how inhuman he looks, how cold. The Sariel I remember was vibrant, always laughing or tearing across the skies. Those were days long before thoughts of rebellion and polluted bloodlines ever divided our ranks.

Once, he was my friend and his wild joy filled our garrison. Now, his face is a desert at nightfall, barren and devoid of all life.

I push past that thought, gracelessly stumbling over my words. "I can't believe what luck I had to find you so quickly! I wasn't sure who I should speak with." Sariel doesn't reply, and my nerve begins to falter under his silent scrutiny.

His outward appearance hasn't changed much in the last few decades. The cut of the light grey suit he wears has modernized, the ash-colored fabric hugging the slim lines of his frame. The coffee brown of his hair is a bit longer, falling against his cheek in waves that soften his appearance.

But his eyes stare through me with a flintiness I've never seen from him, and everything in me screams to put distance between us.

This was a mistake. No one knows where you are, and no one but Michael could follow if they did!

Inside, I'm shaking, and I curse Brielle for reducing me to this. I'm an angel. Men have knelt and wept for their mothers in my presence, but now I struggle to keep my hands from trembling. I smile tightly and force myself to take a step closer to Sariel. I've come too far to run without trying.

"I need your aid, Sariel," I say earnestly, pushing everything I can muster into my words. "A necromancer has torn open portals into Hell, and demons are swarming the Earth. We haven't been able to stop it alone."

My voice trails off when his expression doesn't change.

After so long away I expected to be greeted with questions and even suspicion, but not this blank disdain.

Sariel's eyes darken at my request, his lips pulling back in a sneer to reveal straight white teeth. "Your pet witch isn't strong enough to hold back Hell, so you crawl back here?"

We used to hide away together on quieter days, whiling away afternoons in the warm sunlight until we were summoned for one errand or another. Our tiny rebellions were no more than those of bored children, shirking our duties for a few hours to stretch our wings before slipping back into blind obedience, but even those miniscule acts of dissent scandalized our garrison.

That Sariel is gone, and what's left behind stares at me with disgust in his eyes like I'm some forgotten sin returned to remind him of his past transgressions.

"Do you believe Heaven is blind, Caila?" he snarls. Sariel grabs my arm, the grip just short of painful, and I know he's waiting for me to give him a reason to attack. My body trembles and I want to wrench my arm away from his touch. My silence angers him and his grip tightens, yanking me forward as he demands, "Do you?"

I catch myself, thankful for Elissa's sturdy boots, no matter how much I might miss my heels. Abruptly Sariel shoves me away. Already off balance, I end up sprawled in the dirt.

In this position, Grace would have some pithy quip, Elissa some profanity laced retort.

I say nothing.

"You betrayed us," Sariel continues. I see the glint of cool metal from the cuff of his suit, and I know his weapon's at the ready.

I'm an enemy of Heaven.

I have not fallen, but that hardly matters anymore.

"You're no better than the Fallen," he spits. His blade stays up his sleeve, and his stance is loose, relaxed.

I'm an enemy, but not a threat, it seems.

The thought incenses me, and I shift just enough to feel the weight of my own weapon against the small of my back.

Sariel doesn't pause in his diatribe on my failings. "The Fallen at least had the decency to choose a side, but you. . . what is that saying the humans have? You wanted to have your cake and eat it too?" He chuckles at his own cleverness before continuing. "You think you can wallow with the filth, with the humans and the Fallen and then crawl home when they can no longer protect you?"

Some reaction must have shown on my face, and Sariel bares his teeth in a triumphant smile. "That's right, Heaven knows who you choose to spend your days with. A witch who pledged herself to Hell was bad enough, but then you added Lucifer and his whore to your household." He falls silent for a moment, as though he's so disgusted by my actions that he can't even speak. "She murdered Uriel like a dog, and you call her friend. You are *worse* than fallen."

I hear the soft hiss of metal against cloth as he finally eases his weapon from its sheath. The warm glow of Eden's sunlight glints blindingly bright on the metal, and I hold my breath, waiting for him to realize what he's done.

He drew a weapon upon another angel in Heaven. Not just in Heaven but in Eden. Not since Lucifer and Michael beat each other bloody at Heaven's borders, and Lucifer's devotees started a war in his stead has an angel drawn a weapon on another here.

The realization of just what led to Lucifer's defection and what caused Michael to finally turn his back on his duty slams into me.

Heaven is broken.

I bow my head, tears pricking in my eyes.

"You've spent too much time with the humans if you think tears will bring you mercy," Sariel taunts. In my peripheral vision, I see him take a step closer to me. If I were in my right mind, he might look menacing. I blink, and a tear escapes my eye, trailing down my cheek to fall into the dark soil I'm still prone upon.

It isn't fear. For the first time since I woke up in the darkness, I'm not afraid. The face my nightmare wears certainly isn't Sariel's. My nightmare cloaks herself in silks and has no need for weapons, and even in death, she threatens to undo the world.

Sariel's still prattling on as though I'm a child to be admonished. I hear his words, hear the hatred they carry within them, but they roll off me like water.

My tears are not from fear. They're from sadness and loss of what Heaven once was and what I'm beginning to believe it will never be again.

I glance up at Sariel, and his lips move but his voice slides away, lost in the silence of Eden. He falters briefly under my detached stare, and I idly wonder what he sees when he looks at me.

The grip on his blade is loose. I'm already defeated as far as he's concerned. I draw in a breath as time slows to a crawl around me.

He won't let me leave.

I pull myself to my feet, slipping a hand behind my back to draw my blade into my hand.

Sariel doesn't notice.

"Do you think you'll be rewarded for killing me?" I ask. I feel like I'm watching myself from a thousand miles away. This broken creature taking a hesitating step backward isn't me.

A day ago, I feared that I'd open my eyes and find myself

still chained and that the last few weeks were nothing but a fever dream.

Now, my greatest fear is that I'm awake and that this is all too real.

I rock backward on my feet, trying to put even a few more inches of distance between us. That tiny movement, he notices, and Sariel advances another step, his long stride erasing the distance I created between us.

My hand tightens around the grip of my knife until even the dull edge of the hilt bites into my skin. Sariel blocks my path to the gate. I could fly, but I know he'd overtake me in seconds.

I shut out the memories of racing through the skies at Sariel's heels, our laughter ringing through Heaven as we chased the stars. He always won our races, his dove grey wings tearing through the miles.

Second place won't be enough today.

"I take no joy in your death, Caila, but what you've done can't be forgiven."

"You take no joy in anything." I let the words hang between us as I search his face for any tiny fragment of recognition. How has he changed so completely in a few years?

I almost laugh at the absurdity of my own thought. After all, I barely recognize myself.

He won't let me leave.

No one knows where I am.

No one will save me this time.

Sariel closes the last step between us before I can say anything else. His hands are in my hair, yanking my head back to bare my neck. He's had enough of words and memories.

He wants blood.

My muscles lock up at the memory of Brielle with the chain wrapped around her fingers like a bridle, taunting Elissa with each drop of my blood she spilled, and I can still smell the iron.

I was nothing. In her hands, I barely felt like an angel anymore. I was just meat awaiting the slaughterer's knife.

My story will not end here.

"You have the privilege of dying within Heaven," Sariel adds, raising his blade toward the hollow of my throat. The blade looks like quicksilver in the fading sun. "It's much more than a traitor deserves."

His last word cuts off in a gurgle as I ram my knife between his ribs.

Sariel staggers backward, his face grey with shock as he tries ineffectually to grasp at the blackened metal of the hilt.

Forged in Hell. Another one of Elissa's gifts.

His knees hit the ground, the soil absorbing the sound in a dull thud, his eyes wide with shock.

I hold my breath, waiting for the world around me to erupt in flames for what I've done, but there is only silence.

Eden does not notice.

Sariel slumps to the ground like a broken doll, and I stumble back, my hands shaking.

The light is fading, and the Garden no longer looks like a lovely dream I could lose myself in. I feel the trees watching, their impassive silence judging us both, and I'm beginning to understand how Uriel fell to madness here.

I spread my wings, taking one final look at the beauty surrounding me. I wait for the regret to cripple me. I know I can't ever return. I'm as unwelcome in Heaven as Lucifer himself.

We're on our own. There will be no aid. There's nothing but the six of us to hold back Hell from consuming the world.

I take to the skies, my mind carefully blank but for one thought.

I have to get home.

9

PHENEX

I can't explain why I keep returning here, but night after night I find myself outside these gates, staring through the iron posts at charred wood and broken plaster.

Lucifer and Michael are hunting yet again, wandering the streets in search of whatever infernal flotsam is polluting the city. They both know that their efforts aren't enough to stem the tide forever, but neither of the archangels is accustomed to losing. With every demon they kill, they let themselves believe that we can win.

I know we can't. That certainty should frighten me, but it almost brings me peace.

Hell will end us, or Heaven will. And a growing part of me doesn't care anymore.

I stay outside the gates. I almost want to tear through the rubble, searching through the wreckage to look for some kind of closure. I'm not even sure what I'd be looking for. A body? Some real indication that Brielle is gone and not just laying in wait for the right moment to tighten another noose around my neck?

I can't. Something of Brielle has permeated the walls, the

very grounds of this place, and after that aborted conversation with Lucifer I can't bring myself to take a step closer, nor can I walk away.

Lucifer keeps his distance, regret and self-recrimination on his face every time he looks at me, while I hide from Caila like a coward. I tell myself it's for her own protection, that I don't want to taint her goodness, but I'm a liar.

I'm afraid. I'm so afraid.

She makes me feel again. Numbness was so much easier, so much *safer*. I tell myself that it wasn't her. It could have been anyone. Any port in the storm. But it wasn't anyone else that evil bitch dragged into my cell. It was Caila.

The whys and the hows don't matter anymore. The might have beens will never come to pass. It wasn't anyone else, and in the weeks or months or years in Hell, she was my solace and I hers. My only solace and my greatest agony.

If Brielle had been a Fallen angel, I suspect Hell wouldn't be in chaos now. She would have enjoyed ruling over her own private kingdom, I think, and the souls under her power would weep. Only she could make you feel pity for the damned.

Grace watches me. While Lucifer tries to give me space, she makes no secret of her attention. Those wide grey eyes follow me through her house, and it takes me far too many days to recognize that attentive look as simple caring.

There's no guilt in Grace, no regret, no memories of shared trauma clawing to the surface. This girl with no family and no roots to tie her here beyond a house and a ginger cat built a new family out of Heaven's unwanted children.

And somehow I became a part of it.

If I close my eyes I can still feel the slice of Uriel's blade across my throat, the cut so quick that I barely felt the sting. Before my brain could register what had happened I was on my knees, choking on my own blood. The din of battle around me faded to muffled shouts and crashes. The sharp scent of a dozen liquors spilling across the floor from the shattered bar was abrasive enough to keep me clinging to the edge of consciousness for a few minutes, but even that faded as my life ebbed away.

Not like this. I'm not ready.

I tried to speak, but my mangled throat barely managed a garbled moan. But she heard me. She understood. I felt a touch on my shoulder, the lightest brush of her hand against my jacket, and it was the last thing I felt as I slipped into darkness.

At least I'm not alone at the end.

It was only a few moments later when I awoke, gasping for air through my aching throat before sitting up and taking in the chaos around me. Uriel lay slumped on the floor, stabbed through the throat, his dead eyes staring blankly at the ceiling. A few feet away, Lucifer sat up slowly, bloodied and dazed but no worse for wear. Michael was standing like a statue beside the ruined bar, utterly shell-shocked at the entire scene, but most of all at Grace.

She stood above the unmoving lump of Uriel's body, streaks of drying blood across her hands, and she was the only one out of us who didn't look at least a little amazed at the turn of events. The youngest in the room by thousands of years, but she looked calm. She looked sure.

She caught my eye and smiled, as if to say, *"You got your second chance. Now use it."* Then Lucifer struggled to his feet, and she had eyes only for him.

This is my second chance, and I'm wasting it.

But I can't stop feeling like at any moment it will be ripped away again.

The wreckage of the mansion is just a silent mockery. Once, I was brave enough to take that leap into Hell after Lucifer. Now I tremble at the sight of a burned out husk.

I let Brielle win. I let her break me because it was less painful than continuing to fight.

I pushed Caila away because I knew it would hurt less than having her taken from me.

I take a step back from the gate. The necromancer doesn't emerge from the rubble. The *click click click* of stiletto heels on damp stone is silenced everywhere but my memory.

I survived.

We survived.

Caila doesn't need me to shield her from the darkness anymore. She doesn't need me to fight her battles for her. She needs me to fight for *us*.

I turn my back on what's left of the mansion and walk away, and when the broken walls creak in the breeze, I don't look back.

THE HOUSE IS quiet when I return.

It's too early for Lucifer and Michael to have given up their hunt, which means Grace should still be across town pouring over spellbooks with Elissa and Caila at her side.

The door to my bedroom hangs ajar just enough that I can see the faint glow of lamplight illuminating the shadows. I don't need any light to know who's waiting inside.

The hinges creak as I push the door open, and Caila is curled up on my bed, her arms wrapped around her knees. Her head snaps up when she hears the door, her entire body tense as if waiting for an attack. Caila relaxes when she sees me, but she still looks far more shaken than I've seen her since we returned.

I cross the small room to sit down beside her, stepping over the heavy pair of boots abandoned beside the bed. I take one of her hands in mine. She's shaking. Even in the dim light, I can see the streaks of dried tears on her cheeks.

"Caila?" I ask. "Are you all right?"

Her fingers tighten around mine, and I look down and notice the rusty streaks along her hands. She feels me tense.

"It's not mine."

"A demon?"

She shakes her head but doesn't elaborate. Something has shifted since the last time I saw her, and her whole world seems twisted on its axis. I make no move to pull my hands away from hers, but her fingers still tighten around mine. I stay silent as she struggles for words.

Let me be your anchor.

"The blood. It's Sariel's." Before I can question whether the remnants of Uriel's garrison have descended on Earth to plague us as well, she shakes her head. "I went back. To Heaven."

"You went back?" She flinches at my sharp words for a moment before nodding, her gaze steely.

"We needed their help," she answers, her steady voice leaves no space for arguments. "We still do, but Heaven won't give it. Not when I'm the one asking."

"But you aren't-"

"Fallen?" She laughs at that, her voice hollow. "Apparently what makes you Fallen or what keeps you in Heaven's good graces is all just semantics now." She lets go of my hands and leans back against the overly fluffy pillows that Grace piled on the bed in an effort to make the room feet homey. "Heaven doesn't care for the company I keep," she adds, watching for my reaction.

"The company you keep," I repeat, a sinking feeling twisting my guts at what she's implying. Did Heaven know what we endured at Brielle's hands? Were they watching, enjoying some sick voyeuristic pleasure at seeing our degradation?

Would they have rescued her if I hadn't been there?

"I'm sorry," I murmur, unable to think of anything else to say.

Caila's face changes immediately, sadness and resignation melting into fiery anger. "Don't you dare," she snaps. "You think Heaven disowned me because of just you? Oh, Phenex."

She leans forward and presses her lips against mine, the kiss quick and almost chaste. She reaches for me, brushing her fingertips across my cheek. "I've spent the better part of sixty years trying to keep Uriel from slaughtering Grace's family. I teamed up with a witch who also happens to be the only person in history who kept Michael from toeing the line in Heaven. And when I was captured the Devil and the Last came to my aid." She sighs. "I was marked as a traitor before you ever saw me."

"You sound like you don't regret it."

"I suppose I do." Caila stands up and wanders to the over-stuffed bookshelf, her bare feet silent on the creaky floors. She runs a fingertip over the spines as she scans the titles of the worn paperbacks. She pulls one out at random, the cover a lurid red with a shadowy figure brandishing a knife. "I never knew Grace was so into horror," she mutters, flipping through the yellowed pages. "No wonder she took all of this in stride."

"Caila."

She closes the book, stuffing it back into the vacant spot on the shelf but doesn't turn to me. "I'm sure I'll regret it later. I expect to be a sobbing mess when this really registers." She ducks her head, taking a deep breath. "Sariel was my friend. Once. And I left him for dead." She looks up at me, her face filled with a thousand naked emotions all tangled into one. "I can never go back. I killed someone I used to care about to save my own life, and I'd do it again."

"Lucifer was right," she adds. "Heaven is broken, and it's been that way for a long time."

Standing in a forgotten bedroom, surrounded by the remnants of someone else's life, in someone else's clothes, Caila has never looked stronger or more beautiful. She extends her hands to me, and I know this isn't just another touch that will lead to nothing.

This is a pledge.

"This is my home now. This is my family now. And I'll do whatever I must to keep it safe."

I take her hand, the skin still streaked with blood. She holds me at arm's length, searching my face for any lingering hesitance. It would be easy to fall into each other's arms, to put aside words and thoughts until tomorrow. But tomorrow has a way of turning into never, and neither of us needs any more impulsivity in our lives.

"Why did you choose to fall?" her word choice is deliberate. Whatever the myths of humans and angels surrounding Lucifer might say, he never *chose* to fall.

He was pushed. I wasn't.

"No one but Lucifer ever asked me that," I reply. I'm not stalling. There are many choices in my past that I regret, but despite my irrational bargain with Michael, this was never one of them.

That doesn't mean condensing thousands of years of history into a few sentences is easy.

Caila's eyes stay fixed on mine, her irises black and unreadable in the dim room. It would be easier to look away, to find some meaningless object in the cluttered room to focus my gaze upon.

I don't look away. I've hidden long enough.

"Lucifer," I begin. "You remember how he was in the early

days?" Caila nods. She might not have been one that followed him into perdition, but no angel in Heaven could deny the thrall he held us all in back then. "Everything about him was intoxicating. He never had to persuade me. He wasn't a serpent holding out a shiny apple enticing good little angels to their damnation. He just wanted us to make our own decisions."

I could almost see him gazing down at humanity with scorn, his blindingly white wings catching the midday sun, powerful and brighter than the sun and stars rolled into one. We were surrounded by the perfection of Heaven, and in those days we knew nothing else.

But on the ground the humans clamored for our attention, the constant din of prayers assaulting our ears with demands. Long before they learned to extract the ores from the soil and hammer the raw metal into blades they found other ways of destruction. For each set of hands that healed, we saw three others that sifted through the dust for a convenient rock to cave in another's skull with.

"Worship that?" Lucifer scoffed.

"Rebellion made sense. He offered a choice. Freedom." I closed my eyes. The idea had been so enticing. Freedom. Choice. Free will. I hadn't even known what it really meant. None of us had. Since our creation, we'd followed Heaven's rules in blind obedience, and we'd been happy for it. We knew nothing else.

Then Father created his new toys and too many of us felt forgotten.

"Do you regret it?"

Caila's voice is quiet, and I wonder just how much she knows of Hell beyond the little corner we were locked in. Few angels have entered the halls of the damned, and even fewer have made it back to tell the Heavenly host of what they witnessed there.

Hell was suffering for all those who entered through its gates. The Fallen were tormented as much as the souls. I think that's why so many were so quick to give in. Embracing the darkness is so much simpler than fighting it.

In the beginning, we all did. In those early days of Hell, the rules were nebulous. The gates kept the souls locked in, but the Fallen came and went as we pleased. Lucifer rode with the Horsemen, and we followed at his heels. We grew drunk on the sins of mankind and our own, but one by one the Fallen found the gates barred to them. As they forgot what they had been, Hell became their prison as well.

Anyone can leave Hell if they don't belong there anymore, and those Fallen that reveled in the same sins they once reviled humans for belonged there.

The doors were never closed to me, never locked. All I had ever wanted was freedom, and I felt no remorse in that. I had the freedom, but the other Fallen looked on me with nothing but suspicion for that liberty.

And what of Lucifer? He saw his great dream of free will twisted into a life he never wanted as the warden of every evildoer the Earth spat out. He heard his name twisted and maligned into something he never wanted to be.

Sometimes it's easier to give in to those expectations.

Better to reign in Hell, or so they say.

"Do I regret it?" I echo. I thought I did. I bartered with Michael, betraying my only friend on a vague hope of returning to Heaven, and I barely know why anymore.

Finally, I answer, "No. Not anymore."

When I kiss Caila this time, it isn't in the heat of the moment. My emotions do not get the better of me. The weak light of the single lamp deepens the shadows in the corners of the room, but it's still bright enough that we have nothing left to hide behind.

I kiss her, and I taste the salt of the tears she shed

lingering on her lips. I barely remember Sariel. In my mind, he's nothing more than a streak across the sky. But I think he was joyful back then, needing nothing but the open air and his own wings to feel free.

How we all have changed.

I can't stop looking at her, at the faint flush growing across her cheeks and swell of her bare lips. She looks so different than when she was first tossed into the cell with me. She clothes herself in dark colors, black t-shirts and heavy denim, boots with thick soles that add more inches to her height than the broken heels I met her in ever did.

The jeans are too long, the inches of extra fabric bunching at her ankles. Her dark shirt is just a bit too snug. The poor fit of the clothes made for Elissa's taller, leaner frame does nothing to hide her beauty, and I certainly won't be the one to tell her to give up her armor. Some part of me can't help wanting to see that gilded creature she once was.

Caila pulls me closer, standing on her toes to wrap her arms around me, her short nails scratching my shoulder blades. I press her against the bookcase, the overloaded shelf creaking in protest, and a few displaced paperbacks rain down on us.

I break the kiss as one smacks me in the forehead, and Caila dissolves into giggles at the look of utter indigence I must be sporting.

"Thank goodness Grace went for paperbacks," I mutter before dropping the offending book to the floor with the others and reclaiming Caila's mouth.

Her laughter is silenced, but I still hear it echoing in the room, bringing a lightness back to both of us that has been gone for far too long. She lets go of my shoulders without breaking the kiss, drawing her hands down my chest to pluck at the front of my shirt.

I expect her to yank it open, scattering buttons and

rending fabric. She doesn't. Her delicate fingers find the first buttonhole and she pushes the plastic disc through without looking. She repeats the process with each button, slow and methodical while I pepper her lips with kisses.

There's no need to rush.

The thought hits me with such a jolt that I freeze for a moment, going still as Caila unfastens the last button and my shirt falls open.

That time in Hell, we never knew when Brielle might return with more torments. We never even knew if she was watching us in the unrelenting blackness of our prison. There was no time to savor, to learn what brings the other the greatest pleasure. We weren't even able to undress beyond what was necessary.

I don't regret it, now that I know we're both alive and free and whole. We both needed that connection to survive.

But now? There's no need to rush.

"Phenex?" Her voice is tentative, drawing me back out of the web of memories.

I smile, taking her hands in mine and bringing them to my lips. Her hands were made to heal, not destroy but they still ended up streaked in blood. I kiss each fingertip, and I know I'm not imagining the shiver that goes through her.

I let go of her hands and take a step backward, away from the bookcase that suddenly looks far too precarious for my liking. The room is small enough that it only takes that single step away from the wall to put me in the center. The corners are shadows, the darkness present but no longer threatening. But here is the brightest point of the room where the soft glow of the desk lamp floods the floor like a tiny incandescent sun.

"Come here," I whisper, and Caila follows.

We stand in the center of the room. The bed beckons from a few feet away, but I don't want to lose myself in a tangle of sheets just yet. I don't want pleasure to close our eyes and blot out everything but sensation.

I need to see.

I need to be seen.

Caila's eyes dart to the bed for a moment when I pause. Her head tilts ever so slightly, her forehead creasing as she tries to decipher what's in my mind. It only takes a moment before she's meeting my eyes again, a knowing smile across her lips.

She wasn't any port in the storm.

Free will feels like a joke to me sometimes. We try to scrape together happiness whenever we can, but we still have the puppet masters in Heaven and Hell tugging on our strings.

I'm done dancing for anyone's amusement.

When Caila's hands slip beneath the cloth of my open shirt, I can't hide the shudder that goes through me when those soft hands rest on my shoulders. She stops for an instant, her eyes staring into mine until I nod.

Free consent, freely given.

No desperation, no fear.

Just this.

Caila pushes my shirt off my shoulders, the white fabric fluttering to the floor unnoticed. Her hands move down the length of my arms, her short nails scratching at my skin just enough to awaken my senses, and I realize just how starved for touch I've been.

Her hands continue their slow travels, brushing across the sensitive skin at the crook of my elbow before tracing the veins down my forearm to the thin bones of my wrists.

My fingers twitch as her nails brush my palms, and she takes a step back, breaking contact and putting me at arm's length. I freeze abruptly, gulping down air to try and calm my harsh breathing. I'm not some neophyte angel with no knowledge of the joys of carnal pleasures, yet this brief contact is almost too much for me, and I'm not blind to the way Caila has shied away from even the most casual touches from any of us.

"Yes," she whispers, sensing my hesitance. The word is barely more than a breath in the quiet of the room. If I concentrated hard enough, the noises of the city would filter in – the din of traffic in the distance, the low hum of souls and their constant demands, the creaks of the walls and the groan of the pipes. But inside this tiny space, it all becomes muffled.

All but the two of us.

I reach across the distance between us, curling my fingers under the hem of the plain black t-shirt Caila wears. I peel it upward, the soft cotton clinging to her curves.

The shirt might be another loan from Elissa but what she wears underneath is most definitely not. Instead of the same stark, utilitarian armor, it's a filmy creation of pale blue lace. The fabric is thin as spider silk, and the dark rose of her nipples peeks through the sheer lace.

I drop the shirt on the floor and pull her against me, the surge of lust flooding me almost dizzying.

Pleasure for pleasure's sake has always been enough for me. In Hell, there were so few crumbs of joy that momentary bliss became all we had to cling to. My bed has rarely lacked companionship, but only a few of those trysts ever meant anything beyond slaking my desire with another warm body or blotting out Hell's screams for a few hours.

In Hell, there was certainly never much room for love.

I loved the memory of Heaven and all it had been before the war splintered us all.

I loved Lucifer for the choice he tried to give to us and for loyalty in the broken world we were left with once the dust settled.

Beyond that, it was all just another way to beat back the darkness. And when I slipped through the gates and wandered the world of humans it was much of the same. I never cared or longed for anything more until I felt Brielle's shackles.

I take a deep breath, chasing that memory from my mind, focusing on Caila's warm body in my arms. I run my fingertips across her shoulder blades, feeling the subtle pulse of her wings as they ache to break free. My own throb in recognition.

I lean forward, capturing her lips for a moment before kissing my way down her neck. Memories of that collar snap at my mind, but I push them aside, forgetting cold iron for smooth skin and the rhythm of her heart beating faster against my lips.

She shifts on her feet as I reach the hollow of her throat, and I know this would all be easier on a nice, flat surface, but I'm reluctant to break away from her long enough to take those few steps.

Instead, I brush my lips along the swell of her breast as I drop to my knees in front of her. The delicate lace does nothing to hide her skin from me, and I run my tongue over her nipple, feeling it peak under my touch. Caila's hands search for purchase in the short locks of my hair as a low moan tears itself from her throat.

My hand finds her other breast, my fingers following the patterns in the lace until they find that same hard peak. Caila trembles under the onslaught, her thighs shaking just the slightest bit. I smile against her skin, and I know she feels it.

My jeans are already uncomfortably tight, and while a small part of me wants to be done with the teasing and bury myself in her warmth, a much bigger part of me knows that this is just the start.

I pull back just enough to kiss the valley between her

breasts before I give the same treatment to the other side. My mouth finds that lace-covered peak, tasting the tantalizing slivers of her skin that the lace can't fully hide until she's gasping my name.

I trail one of my hands down her stomach, the muscles contracting at the light touch, and I pause with my hand on the button of her borrowed jeans. The moment stretches in between us as I look up to meet her eyes.

Caila already looks wrung out, arousal swallowing up the brown of her eyes. She nods, just the slightest tilt of her head, but it's enough. I don't break her gaze when I unfasten the button and draw the zipper down.

Through the open V of her jeans, I can see just a hint of the same light blue fabric, and I dip my hand inside. My fingertips brush against the same soft lace, and Caila's knees almost buckle as my touch presses the damp lace against her sensitive skin.

It's too much of a temptation, and we're both still far too clothed so I ease my hand out and tug the jeans down over her hips. The worn black denim pools at her feet, and she rests one hand on my shoulder as she delicately steps out of them before kicking them away.

I sit back on my heels and just stare at her. I've never seen her like this. Clothed in nothing more than filmy lingerie that hides nothing, she looks calmer than she ever did wrapped in layers of clothing to shield herself.

As enticing as the sky blue lace is though, it's still too much.

"Take it off," I say. My voice comes out as a choked rasp, but it's far from a command.

Let me see you. Let me see all of you.

Caila reaches a hand behind her and unfastens the bra, pushing the straps off her shoulders and dropping it carelessly to the floor. A moment later, the last bit of lace joins it on the floor, and she's bare before me.

The pale gold of her hair only just brushes her collarbone, but she still sweeps it out of the way before extending her hand to me. "Stand up," she breathes.

I do. I can't stop looking at her. I've seen beauty in every form, tasted the fruits of the loveliest that creation has to offer. I've watched their bodies flush with pleasure and lost myself in their skin against my own.

None of it compares to what I see before me when I look at Caila.

Her hands rest at my waist, and I nod without prompting, ready to be rid of this last barrier between us. The heel of her hand brushes against the bulge stretching the denim, and it's my turn to tremble under her touch. My hips thrust against her hands, as she massages me lazily through my jeans, the gentle squeezes just enough to be maddening.

"I like having you at my mercy," she murmurs, finally relenting and easing the zipper down.

Caila wastes no more time teasing. The pants are just an impediment now, and she drags them down my thighs to kneel at my feet.

It should look awkward or at the very least profane, but as Caila kneels nude before me I can't think of her as anything but what she is. Whatever her choices or actions, there's nothing fallen about her.

She unties the laces of my boots one at a time, watching me with those unreadable eyes as I toe them off, adding the boots along with my pants to the growing pile of discarded clothing on the floor.

"Stand up." I offer her my hand, repeating her earlier words, but Caila ignores it. Her lips brush the inside of my knee, pausing just long enough to nip the skin before she presses an open-mouthed kiss to my inner thigh, dragging her lips shut and drawing out the sensation until I'm light-headed.

"Caila," I groan. My voice sounds like a stranger's, some shattered creature lost in a haze of pleasure. I try to say her name again, but the word is strangled in my throat when her lips brush the side of my cock as she continues upward.

She doesn't stop, dragging her tongue up my length before pressing another wet kiss on my hip. She rises slowly to her feet then, drawing her nails across my ribs hard enough to raise thin red lines that fade an instant later.

Finally upright, Caila takes a step away from me, giving my body the same look of fevered reverence I gave her.

There's nothing left to hide behind anymore for either of us.

The smoldering heat that's been brewing between us is suddenly too much. I scoop her up in my arms as the heat boils over.

It's barely two steps to the bed, and we collapse grace-lessly onto the narrow mattress. We're a tangle of limbs, and a giggle breaks free from Caila's throat as the wooden frame creaks under our weight. This small bed wasn't meant to contain the antics of two angels.

I end up reclined on the mattress with Caila above me, and I can't hold back the hum of appreciation as her thighs fall to either side of my hips. Her hand rests flat against my chest, my heartbeat pounding against her palm.

We've been here before. Desperate and aroused, taking what comfort we could find in the darkness. If I closed my eyes, I could feel the whisper of Caila's skirt against my thighs and the unforgiving stone under my back. So I keep them open.

Caila shifts her hips, and that little bit of friction rips a gasp out of my throat. She goes still, drawing out these last moments of anticipation, and I keep my eyes open and focused on her face as she sinks down onto me.

The heady pleasure hits me like a punch. Sex is nothing new. I've lost count of the lovers I've had over the centuries, forgotten most of their names if I knew them in the first place. Eventually, they all become a blur of skin - soft curves and hard angles, salt and sweat and *sensation*.

It's almost too much, her warmth tightening around me, and the thought that I just might love her tumbles into my mind.

"Phenex." She says my name in one long, drawn-out breath. Caila looks lost, drunk in pleasure, and I suddenly need more. I yank her against me, pulling her down against my chest in an attempt to get as close as possible.

It's a bad angle, and we both know it, but if Caila has any objections to the abrupt move she doesn't show it. She catches my lower lip between her teeth, the nip playful and the words spill from me before I can hold them back.

"I love you." They come out as a whisper against her lips. It would be easy to pass them off as a sigh of pleasure, to blame them on the heat of the moment, to ignore them.

Caila pulls back, barely an inch from me. We're nose to nose, and the look in her eyes tells me all I need to know.

Then she brings her lips to my ear and murmurs, "I love you too."

No one ever could. No one ever has.

But she does.

Caila sits up and pulls me with her. Her lips trace my jaw before pressing against the ugly scar across my throat as her hips start a faster rhythm.

It feels like flying.

I tighten my arms around her back, rocking my hips against hers. My whole body reaches out towards her, desperate for more. The sweet lure of release is already building, and I never thought I'd find my way here, brought to my knees by another and grateful for it.

Caila's nails bite into my shoulder as her inner muscles tighten around me when she breaks. The slow heat that has built and built since I pushed open the bedroom door finally overtakes us both. Caila tilts her head back, a throaty cry of ecstasy escaping her as her body shudders around me.

My arms slip down to her waist, my breath stalling in my lungs as I thrust deeper into her. The pressure winds tighter and tighter until I feel like I'm ready to snap, but it's the low whisper of my name on her lips that finally undoes me.

We're both lost in the afterglow and each other. The literal forces of Hell could be pounding at the door, but I doubt we'd hear them.

Sleep is the last thing on my mind, but I still settle back onto the mattress, pulling Caila with me. Her head rests on my chest, the beat of my heart a slowing rhythm in her ear. Her hand finds mine, her fingers tightening as I let my eyes slip shut, secure in the knowledge that she'll still be there when I open them.

10

CAILA

I don't sleep.

Phenex dozes beside me, and I can feel the thrall of sleep plucking at the edge of my consciousness, but I fight it.

Neither of us needs to rest, not really. Unless we're injured, angels don't require anything as mundane or human as sleep. Most of us are glad of that fact. Over the centuries, I've listened to more than a few of my siblings mock the humans for frittering away their brief lifespans in slumber.

It still seems a waste to me. Humans have so few years in this world. They lose a handful to childhood and an even larger chunk to the decay of old age. I can't imagine giving up a full third of my limited days to unconsciousness.

But even those of us that don't need slumber find ourselves slipping into the habit of sleep out of boredom or merely the comfort of a soft mattress.

Or the right companion.

I didn't expect this.

I expected comfort and pleasure. Maybe even healing.

Not a declaration of love from the Second Fallen.

There was such shock on his face when he spoke those words, but buried under that surprise was an even deeper well of fear. And all of that was overshadowed with utter disbelief at my reply.

He expected pity. He expected me to see him as just a convenient body to chase away the nightmares.

In the very beginning, he might have even been right.

There's no escaping our origin. Whatever exists between us was forged in blood and pain and Hellfire as surely as the blackened metal of our daggers.

I've bled for him, and he for me, and I suspect it won't be the last time.

Hell is still waiting outside these walls, and my actions tonight won't escape Heaven's notice.

I don't want dawn to come and remind me of that yet, so I stay awake and watch him breathe.

"Talk."

Despite my fervent wishes, dawn did come and with it another day of fruitless searching. Only today when I unlock my front door I'm not greeted with an empty room or a precarious pile of spellbooks strewn across the coffee table. Elissa sits perched on the grey velvet sofa, a cup of coffee that could double as a cereal bowl in her hand. She glances up at the click of the door, one dark eyebrow arching as she takes in my appearance. There's no hiding last night's wrinkled clothes and tangled hair.

Her face breaks into a grin an instant after the realization of just why I look so disheveled hits her. It's almost as though the last few weeks have never happened, and it's just the two of us trying to save our little corner of the world again.

"Staying out all night with a boy? Caila, what will people

think?" Elissa takes a dramatic sip of her coffee, and I can't help smiling back. She sounds lighter than she has in ages, and I feel it too. The sword is still hanging above all of our heads, but for just a few minutes it's tempting to forget.

This girl smirking as she teases me about my walk of shame feels more like the Elissa I've known for years than the strained, stressed mess she's been since I returned.

I've barely settled onto the sofa beside her, ready to steal a few moments before we get to work when Grace enters through the unlocked door behind me. An oversized cup of coffee is in her hand as well, and her face wears the same perpetual look of bone-deep exhaustion we all do.

Human or not, we're all feeling the strain.

Something has to give and soon.

Grace falters as she steps inside the room, closing the door behind her with a quiet click. She pauses in the entry-way, shifting from one foot to the other as she takes us both in. She looks almost shy.

It's easy to forget that out of all of us, she's the one true outsider. The angels have eons of history between us. Even Elissa and I have spent decades living in each others' pockets as we crisscrossed the country.

For all that she fit herself into the jagged jigsaw puzzle of our ensnared lives, Grace is still the newest piece, and that realization catches her by surprise at the strangest times.

My own words to Phenex echo in my head. *This is my home now. This is my family now. And I'll do whatever I must to keep it safe.*

Hiding the truth behind guilt and shame never kept anyone safe.

Elissa tilts her head at Grace, a lazy smile across her lips. At least for the moment, Elissa seems to have decided that the brewing apocalypse can wait, and I'm thankful for the reprieve, however short it might be.

"Grab a chair, Grace," Elissa says, propping one booted foot up on the coffee table, pointedly ignoring my eye-roll. "Caila was just about to tell us about her night. Weren't you Caila?"

Grace's eyes flit from me to Elissa and back again before she pulls the same sly smile Elissa wears.

"About damn time," she says, settling into one of the armchairs. "The two of you have been dancing around each other for long enough."

Elissa doesn't bother to hide a snort of laughter, and the awkwardness of a moment ago dissipates as if it never existed.

"But seriously," Grace adds softly once the laughter has faded away. "I'm happy for you two. At first, I wasn't sure if he'd come out of it at all." We fall silent as Grace gives voice to the words none of us could help thinking when this all started.

"Lucifer didn't say much, but I know seeing Phenex like that was hard for him," Grace continues. "I think he blamed himself for a lot of it."

Elissa sighs, her relaxation gone as the all too familiar shutters slam over her eyes. "Join the club."

"This wasn't your fault." I reply without hesitation, and Elissa's sad smile is enough for me to shake my head at her, repeating with vehemence, "This. Is not. Your fault."

"Fine."

A few days ago, I would have accepted that. I would have given her an out and let us both bury the guilt and shame and regret as though hiding it would erase it from existence.

Nothing stays buried. Not in our lives.

"No," I snap. "Not fine." I reach for Elissa and take the cup from her hand, putting it down on the coffee table hard enough that a few dark drops spill over the side to pool on the wood. I know that without anything else to occupy her,

Elissa will either get up and stalk away or she'll actually look at me.

Luck is on my side for once, and Elissa lets her ice blue eyes drift upward to meet mine.

It's like a dam breaking. The words rush out of her, her voice cracking as she fights to rein in the flood of emotions. "I brought this on all of us, Caila. Michael gave the order. Raziel killed Roux, but I started it. If it hadn't been for me and the things I taught her, Brielle wouldn't have survived that fire, and none of this would have happened."

Elissa swipes her hand across her eyes, and I pretend not to see the moisture gathered there. "And I hate her for what she did to you and to Phenex, but part of me. . ." Her voice trails off into nothing, and she stares down at her clenched hands resting in her lap as though they held the answers.

"You cared about her," Grace offers.

"I cared about both of them," Elissa corrects. "There was no malice in either of them when we were together. Michael called them 'small-time grifters with just enough power and nobility to get what they wanted.'" Elissa shakes her head at those words, tucking a few strands of her dark hair behind her ear before daring a glance back up at me. "Being with the two of them was *fun*. They didn't want anything to do with Heaven or Hell. They just wanted to enjoy everything the world had to offer them."

A ghost of a smile crosses Elissa's face at that. She's had so little real, uncomplicated happiness in her life, and it only makes me hate Brielle more for tainting those memories.

"Life was just one long party. We shared everything. Magic. Power. Each other."

There it is. I'd suspected as much. Once you rack up more than a few centuries of life more and more of the restrictions that the world of man seems to love so much fall away.

Little shocks me anymore. Certainly not this.

Elissa's cuts her eyes between the two of us, trying to appraise our reactions for a moment before giving up and pushing on. "It wasn't love," she whispers. "Even then, even after all that time had passed I didn't have it in me after Michael. But for a little while, I was happy, and I grieved for them both." Elissa takes a deep breath, sinking back into the sofa cushions and staring straight ahead. "It's hard not to hate yourself a little bit when you feel sad that the person who tortured your best friend is dead."

The silence hangs heavy in the room after that. Elissa's hands twitch in her lap, and I know she's moments away from jumping up. She'll be out the front door and tearing down the street on that bike before I can blink, burying this conversation behind sarcasm and a faked smile while it eats away at her.

I put a stop to that before she can start down that path again. Shifting in my seat to face her, I take Elissa's hands in mine, pretending not to notice the tiny tremors. "We all have a past. We all have things we regret." I look over at Grace and feel the familiar twist in my chest. "We all have things we've failed at."

Elissa follows my gaze and shakes her head. "That's not the same," she hisses.

"Isn't it?"

"Care to enlighten me?" Of course, she noticed. Grace is far from stupid, and I know I've been less than subtle in my avoidance of her. I can't very well berate Elissa for her misplaced guilt while still clinging to mine.

What's the old saying? Tell the truth and shame the Devil?

The Devil isn't here. All that's here right now is the three of us and too many memories.

CALIFORNIA
1964

SERAFINE HASN'T CHANGED.

That hard edge in her eyes was already present at our first meeting, put in place by her mother's imprisonment and her father's cruelty. But it was Milly's death that honed that edge to razor sharp steel.

No one was more surprised than Serafine herself when Dean Anderson slipped past all her defenses with his ocean blue eyes and his easy smile.

Dean was every bit the all American boy that the 60s so loved to glorify. Born and raised in the California sunshine in a city where nothing seemed older than a decade, Dean offered a chance for Serafine to put aside the memories of fire and blood that haunted her every night.

They met where everyone seemed to meet in that golden city. The relentless silence drove Serafine out of her apartment and onto the pier. Surrounded by the crowds of cheerful vacationers with the warm salt air around her, Serafine could let herself live that illusory dream of a normal life.

Every afternoon she'd wander up and down the wooden slats of the pier, breathing in the fresh salt of the ocean mixed with the savory scents of fried food from the hot dog carts. When the sun began its descent, she'd sit on a bench and stare out over the ocean, watching as the impossibly blue depths faded from bright turquoise to dull navy and finally black.

One of those days, Dean sat beside her. He said nothing beyond a murmured, "hello." Instead, he sat in easy silence next to her, watching as the day slipped into twilight, and when Serafine stood up to make her way home, he didn't follow.

But he was waiting on the same bench the next evening.

Life had taught Serafine to be suspicious. If she knew I was still hovering at the periphery of her life like a celestial bodyguard, she didn't let on. When she sat down on the bench for the third day, her pockets bulged with charms and her hair still smelled faintly of the herbs she'd burned to refresh the wards Elissa had woven around her.

When he showed no reaction to that protective magic blanketing her, Serafine breathed a sigh of relief without even understanding why she cared.

On the fourth day, she told him her name and asked why he was sitting on the same bench every afternoon.

Dean Anderson smiled and replied, "I wanted to see what you were seeing."

Soon enough, they were driving along the coast with the wind whipping through Dean's black convertible. From there the world of vengeful angels and protection spells began to seem very far away, and bit by bit the twisted snarl of knots that called itself Serafine's soul started to unravel.

The scenery raced by, from the dizzying heights of the cliffs to the ocean crashing against the rocks below. The hairpin turns along the Pacific Coast Highway didn't scare Serafine, and heights had never bothered her, but the wild scenery was still enough of a flimsy excuse to press herself against Dean's side on the bench seats.

On the seventh day, they watched the sunset by Morro Bay, and the woman who trusted no one started to fall in love.

IT WAS BARELY six months later when Dean got down on one knee beside their bench, but Serafine didn't hesitate. It was a rare cloudy day, but the sun was still bright enough to make the ruby ring he slipped onto her finger sparkle. As the crowd of onlookers clapped for the happy couple, Serafine could almost let herself believe that her family curse had been left behind for good.

Serafine was many things, but a capable liar was not one of them.

I kept my distance. The memories still dogged me of how complete my failure to protect my charge had been. If I'd been unable to protect Milly from another human, how did I expect to shield Serafine from Uriel?

I watched through plate glass windows as she tried on white dresses alone, twirling in yards of rustling satin in front of a tall mirror while the shopkeepers cooed over what an absolute vision she was. Serafine let them drape her in lace, but something in her smile looked hollow, and the shadows that Dean had chased away in these past few months seemed to already be creeping back into her eyes.

She'd allowed herself to get lost in this carefree California dream she'd adopted as her own, but the weight of that ring on her finger had snapped her back to reality.

She might be able to change coastlines, but her family was still cursed.

And Dean had no idea of the centuries of baggage his future wife had tethered to her back.

It was written across her face as plainly as could be. If she brought Dean deeper into this world would he begin to regret the day on the pier and every day after?

"I know you're there."

I followed Serafine home from the bridal shop, keeping my usual vigil outside her apartment as though my presence would be enough to deter an archangel.

The soft words drift out through the open window. She left the front door unlocked. A lock certainly couldn't keep out anyone that might be hunting her, but I appreciate the gesture nonetheless.

Little has changed in the apartment in the months since I

was last invited inside. The lemon tree by the front door has perked up, the scraggly leaves thickening and growing glossy emerald in the warm weather. Two lemons dangle from the branch closest to the door, fat with tart juices.

The broken doorknob has long since been replaced, and a second heavy deadbolt flanks it. A bright brass chain dangling down the inside of the door rounds out the trio. Uriel would laugh at those useless mortal locks, but I'm not oblivious to the comfort she must get from the illusion of security.

After all, it wasn't an angel that took her friend.

In two steps the narrow entryway opens up to the living room. The mint green carpeting that covered the floors has long since been torn up. Milly's blood had soaked through to the floorboards, and no amount of carpet shampoo could have lifted that stain. The landlord replaced it with a baby blue that would be just as useless as it's predecessor at hiding bloodstains.

I wonder if Serafine had that same thought.

A few feet away is the darkened rectangle of another hallway leading to the bedrooms. The door that once led to Milly's is firmly shut. The apartment is like a funhouse copy of what it had been, so similar that the tiny changes leave it feeling off.

The bright floral sofa still dominates the small living room, and there sits Serafine, watching me lose myself in those dark memories.

Mixed in among the sameness are pieces of Dean scattered like breadcrumbs through the house – an empty beer bottle resting on the kitchen counter, a pair of men's shoes by the back door, a photograph of the happy couple grinning in the bright sun tucked into the mirror in the entryway.

"I'm always here."

I expect Serafine to be angry at that admission. She ran a thousand miles to escape Heaven and find her freedom, but she can't forget who and what she is with her own angelic shadow. But whatever her wishes, I just can't walk away and leave her to the whims of fate and Uriel.

Instead, she pats the cushion beside her, welcoming me back into her life like an old friend. "Should I be expecting Elissa to pay a visit as well?" she asks.

I sit. Just as before, it's too easy to let myself be lulled by her presence. She feels like a curious mix of humanity and *home*. It makes sense, but I'm not here to be comforted.

"She's around."

Serafine toys with the cigarette in her hand while she watches me. It stays unlit this time. The appeal of watching it burn to a column of ash seems to have faded.

"They named him William," she says without preamble, tossing the still unlit cigarette back into the pristine ashtray. "Milly's parents did. Her brother is raising him. He has a wife. A daughter. It's a ready-made family." Serafine smiles sadly at that. "They live in Boston, so I'll probably never see him again." Serafine looks down at her hands when she adds. "It's better this way. Sometimes not knowing is better."

I already knew, but I keep silent. The boy may not have been my charge, but just as I'd been unable to walk away from Serafine, I'd kept tabs on the child. While I'd stayed in California in the aftermath, Elissa made the long trek back east following a few steps behind the heartbroken couple meeting their grandson for the first time.

Little Will Murphy would grow up far from the madness and cruelty that had surrounded his birth. He didn't need angels or witches watching over him anymore, but Elissa hadn't been able to resist weaving a cloak of protections around the boy before she left him.

Serafine runs her fingertip across her ring. Outside the crimson orb of the sun is already dipping below the bright blue of the Pacific, and in the growing shadows of the room, the stone on her finger looks almost black.

"I know I need to tell him," she whispers. "I know it's not over."

I want to lie to her. I want nothing more than to swear that I'll lay down my life to set her free, but false security won't save her from Uriel's blade.

I say nothing. She doesn't need my advice on this. She knows what needs to be done.

SERAFINE'S CALIFORNIA boy surprised us all.

He believed her.

Even more surprising, he never faltered in his devotion.

A month later, I stood with Elissa watching as a barefoot Serafine married Dean Anderson on the beach. Neither of them could stop smiling long enough for a proper kiss, and as soon as the words "I now pronounce you man and wife" left the young reverend's mouth they were running to the water, laughing as the frothy white waves swirled around Serafine's skirt.

It was a good day.

I stayed. I hung back at the edges of their lives, watching their simple, human joy at building a life from nothing.

And on a rainy afternoon in September, barely a year after watching them laughing on the beach they welcomed Marianne into the world.

Beautiful, stubborn Marianne. Born with her eyes open, staring into the world as if daring it to defy her. Serafine went a bit mad in those first days after her birth, begging Elissa to double and redouble the wards on her house.

Elissa did as she asked without hesitation. She'd suffered

too much under Heaven's thumb herself to be lax in her protections.

Two years passed in an eyeblink since that fateful day we all fell into each other's lives in the lobby of the Casa del Mar, but I still keep Michael's name out of my vocabulary, just as Elissa never asks just why I'm defying my garrison to shield Serafine and her family.

The years fall away like days. It's been quiet here in the little apartment by the beach. Marianne grows from a squalling infant to a bright-eyed inquisitive child, and Elissa and I are never far away, watching her like two eccentric aunts.

Until the day Serafine tells us both that she intends to return to New Orleans.

"I need to prepare her." The shadows creep up the walls of the apartment. A single bulb glows above the stove, and this feels clandestine, like the spy novels Dean leaves in teetering piles on the coffee table.

The door to Milly's old bedroom is still firmly closed, but now a bright square of construction paper with MARIANNE scrawled in blue crayon in a child's shaky hand decorates the wood.

Dean leans against the kitchen counter, listening in silence as Serafine talks of uprooting their picture-perfect life.

"We all know what's coming." Serafine abandoned the hairspray and pin curls ages ago, and her hair falls in soft gold waves around her shoulders. In the low light, she looks much younger than she is, but she doesn't look afraid.

"I need to prepare her. I won't have her stumbling through her future like I did." She looks up at Dean, the love in her eyes such a palpable force that I feel like an intruder. "I have what my mother never had. Allies. Maybe we can win. Maybe we can end this curse once and for all." The hope shines across her face for a moment, and I want so badly to believe it's the truth. Then it shifts into realism as quickly as shutter slamming in a hurricane.

She doesn't believe we'll win.

I don't know how I never saw it until now. When Milly's husband tore into this house and knocked her out, some part of Serafine never got up. She knew the life she carved for herself was built on sand, and she can already feel the tides rushing in.

YEARS PASS. Elissa and I make our own way across the country, crisscrossing the states, stopping for weeks or months at a time to lend what aid we can. We feel Heaven's thumb bearing down on us as we carve out our own path across the country. Neither of us says it, but we see Milly and Serafine in every woman we meet, see Will and Marianne in every child.

And we're always ready to be summoned back to New Orleans at a moment's notice.

Even without getting that call, we find excuses to visit the city, keeping watch from a distance.

Nine-year-old Marianne, gangly as a colt, climbing the ancient oak in her parents' backyard, trying to catch up to the older boy two limbs above her.

"Wait for me, Will!"

Turns out we weren't the only ones to hear the call of the Crescent City.

Little Will Murphy has grown. Only a few days shy of eleven years old, he and Marianne are inseparable. As the bakery grew to be too much for Milly's aging parents to manage on their own, their prodigal son returned, bringing along a wife, a teenaged daughter, and Will.

The elderly couple welcomed Serafine back into their lives

like a missing daughter with no talk of guilt or blame. And when Serafine met the quiet boy for the first time since that terrible day that marked his birth, she could almost believe he recognized her.

It seemed to be woven into their DNA. Marianne and Will were thick as thieves, and as the years passed no one was surprised when it grew into more.

Marianne lived a double life, listening in rapt attention as her mother drilled protection spells and intricate wardings into her teenaged mind, teaching her the real history of their family and where they fit into the worlds of Heaven and Hell.

Erzulie claimed another space in young Marianne's life. The lone ally of her grandmother and the one who'd taught her mother the truth of the Celestin bloodline, the loa educated Marianne in the intricacies of voodoo.

Marianne took to Erzulie's teachings far more than she ever did to Elissa's incantations and sigils. The teenager would disappear into the swamps with Erzulie, cutting herbs and stitching together mojo bags, and then just like a double agent in the spy novels her father still devoured, she'd shed that Marianne for another. This Marianne was a happy normal girl who used that same ancient oak she climbed as a child as an escape route, sneaking out of her house to steal kisses with Will Murphy.

That all ended the summer Marianne turned sixteen.

It wasn't an angel or a demon. It wasn't a spell that went awry.

It was just someone looking away for a moment as they drove through a crosswalk.

It was stupid and human and it happened far too fast.

Dean never even saw the car.

Marianne tossed the carefully harvested herbs and meticulously assembled mojo bags into the fireplace. The blaze burned bright, heating the already warm house to scorching while Serafine stared numbly into the flames.

When Marianne rushed out the back door to cry into Will Murphy's shoulder, leaving her silent mother surrounded by the sharp scent of her bonfire, Serafine let her go.

"Serafine." Elissa's touch on her shoulder didn't rouse her. The flue had been closed tight for the summer, and Marianne's half-hearted attempt to wrench it open hadn't been enough. The smoke drifted back into the room like a haze, the familiar cleansing scent of the burning herbs lost under the scorched fabric smell of the mojo bags.

Sighing, Elissa left her side to pry open the windows, hoping for a breeze to chase the smoke outside but the air was still. None of us had the heart to douse Marianne's blaze.

"I did this."

Serafine's words were little more than a whisper. For all that I wanted to assure her she was wrong and that it was an accident and not Heaven's manipulations, even now I'm still not sure.

We're all nothing but chess pieces on a board. Who's to say Dean wasn't another pawn?

SERAFINE SHOCKED us all by living long enough to see her granddaughter's entrance into the world. Grace came into the world in the unrelenting heat of August, and we all held our breath that day.

Elissa and I expect the night to end in fire and blood rained down from Heaven's wrath. The scene before us is too happy, too perfect for Uriel to allow it to stand. An exhausted Marianne cradles the tiny bundle to her chest while Will strokes her sweaty hair. Serafine sits at the edge of her bed, watching the new family with a small smile on her face.

She'd never dared to hope for this. She still doesn't entirely believe it, but she's going to cling to this happiness for as long as she can.

"Grace," Marianne whispers, her voice rough and tired. "We'll call her Grace."

"No."

Marianne stands beside the white lacquered bassinet, her arms crossed as she glares at me.

"No," she repeats, shaking her head, the messy curls bouncing with her movement. "You seriously think I'm going to uproot my entire life and run away? Are you insane?" Grace stirs in her bed, the soft blanket rustling with her movement, and Marianne lowers her voice. "I told you, I'm *done* with all of this," she hisses. She rounds on Elissa, "*Your* magic couldn't save my father." Then her ire turns to me, "And neither could *your* Heaven."

Marianne crosses her arms across her chest and glares at us both, her gaze cold enough to freeze an ocean.

"I think you both should leave."

"Marianne, please-" Serafine stands up, trying to interrupt her daughter's tirade, but Marianne jerks her head to the left to fix her mother with the same unrelenting look.

"No, Mom." Some of the anger drains out of Marianne when faced with her mother's concern, but she's still just as resolute. "I'm not leaving my home. What would I even tell Will?"

"The truth?" Serafine offers. "I told your father the truth. It was hard and scary and the last thing I wanted to do, but I told him."

"Will isn't Daddy," Marianne snaps back. "I don't want him to know about any of this. *I* don't want to know about any of this. I just want to have a normal life, and I can't do that with a witch and an angel hovering around me. Please, just go."

A few moments later, Serafine is shepherding us out the front door and standing on the sidewalk with us. "You feel it too, don't you?" she asks, staring down the ribbon of asphalt as though expecting Uriel to pull up in a cab. "It's in the air. It has been ever since Grace was born."

Serafine turns to me, and I'm surprised to see tears gathered in the corners of her eyes. I've never seen Serafine cry. She weathered the deaths of her best friend and her husband in quiet numbness, her agony more palpable than if she had wailed her loss aloud, but her eyes stayed dry. Then she blinks, and she's nothing but steely resolve again. "She's the one, isn't she?"

I nod, finally admitting what we'd all known since Grace took her first breath. "She's the Last."

"So I don't have long." Serafine's words are so matter-of-fact it's almost jarring, but we all know she's right. Word of her birth will reach Heaven soon enough, if it hasn't already, and any angel that sees her will instantly know that she's something more than just another human.

"I have a plan."

We stand in the shadow of Marianne's perfect little house and plot.

TEN MONTHS.

For ten months we weave spells into a tapestry around Serafine, but these aren't the same benevolent protections that cloak Marianne and Grace inside their happy home.

These are darker. These are the spells that demand a sacrifice, that demand blood. We carve them into the floorboards of Serafine's house and paint them in ashes across the walls. Serafine slaps a fresh layer of wallpaper over them to keep up appearances and hides the marks on the floors under brightly colored rugs. The underside of every chair, every table, even the bottoms of her kitchen cabinets are etched with sigils and scarred with Enochian.

To say nothing of Serafine herself.

This spell wants blood. It wants pain, and it wants a sacrifice.

When Elissa drew the symbols on the pale skin of Serafine's forearms, she watched the whorls and curves take shape on her skin.

When Elissa handed her the knife and told her to carve the markings into her own flesh, she didn't hesitate, and we all felt life slide into the spell as smoothly as a chambered bullet.

Serafine wears long sleeves after that to hide the healing wounds and the scars they leave in their wake.

And we wait.

We built a bomb.

And I'm not there when it explodes.

Serafine is fifty years old, and Grace is three weeks shy of turning one when Uriel comes to call.

And I can't be there.

Every angel within miles will be caught in the fallout, and we all know that we'll be lucky if we have minutes to spare when the time comes.

My presence is a liability, so I stay away.

I squeeze Serafine's hand that night when we put the final touches on the spell, and we both know it's goodbye. Twenty-five years is a second to me, but it's half her life. She's still the same spitfire who didn't hesitate to attack me outside a dress shop. Some of her edges have been worn down by love and loss, but beneath it all, there's still steel.

Serafine is ready, and she has no regrets.

At least I know she won't be alone at the end.

When Uriel tears into Serafine's quiet house, Elissa is waiting in the shadows like a guard dog, and the two women snap their trap around the archangel.

Elissa told me later that Uriel advanced on her, snarling his usual half-crazed words about ending her tainted bloodline. Serafine stared down at the archangel that had tormented her family for generations without flinching.

She didn't hesitate as she sliced one of Elissa's Hell-forged knives across her forearm, making the cut deep enough that blood started pouring in seconds.

She looked at Uriel, at the angel that caused her mother's death as surely as if he had pushed her off that roof himself, and she whispered the Enochian words that would activate the spell.

And she smiled.

Elissa didn't see much else after that. She sprinted out the front door and down the freshly swept brick stairs, trying to put as much distance as she could between herself and the front door.

The shock wave from the explosion was enough to knock her to the ground, the jolt from hitting the sidewalk rattling her teeth as her ears rang.

Dazed, she stood up a moment later to see that the house had been reduced to little more than a smoking crater.

Curious neighbors started poking their heads out their front doors before the echo of the explosion had fully faded. Someone yelled about calling the fire department, but all Elissa could do was stare at the wreckage and hope that Uriel wouldn't emerge from it.

He didn't. It worked.

He wasn't dead, but Serafine had bought a chance for her daughter and her granddaughter with her life.

This wouldn't be the first fire Serafine lit.

SERAFINE HAD HIDDEN AWAY everything that mattered to her with me. Half a dozen boxes, loaded with books and photos, trinkets and memories.

And a letter.

I didn't read it. I didn't need to. We showed up at Marianne's doorstep while the flames of the house she had grown up in still smoldered.

Will was away on a work trip. Marianne narrowed her eyes at the sight of both of us, but stepped aside and invited us in.

"What's going on?" she demanded. "Did my mother send you two to try and talk more sense into me?"

I shake my head and press the envelope into her hand, sinking down onto the velvet sofa that Serafine always teased her about as being so impractical with a small child.

I hear Marianne's voice catch on a sob as she reads, and she looks at both of us, accusations written across her face. "You let her do this? You *helped* her do this?"

"It was the only way."

"You're an angel!" She whirled on Elissa. "You're a freaking immortal witch. What good have either of you ever done for us?"

A thin cry comes from down the hall, and Marianne turns her back on us to tend to Grace. She stops in the doorway and turns to us with a tear-streaked face.

"Get out." Her hand clenches the doorway, and Serafine's letter crumples under her grip. "Stay away from me, and stay away from my family."

This time, we listen.

THE YEARS dull Marianne's rage, but she still can't stand to look at us. She turns to Erzulie, to the memories of disappearing into the swamps, and bit by bit she slips back into that version of Marianne. She strings bunches of herbs from the rafters and scrawls veves in chalk on the undersides of all her furniture. She sews charms into the linings of all her purses and stuffs mojo bags under the seats of the family car.

She avoids churches.

Grace grows into a happy, strong-willed teenager with no awareness of the forces circling her, and after too many years I stop caring about preserving Marianne's idyllic life.

"You have to tell her," I beg into the cold plastic of the telephone receiver. "She can't go into all this blind. It needs to come from you."

Age has softened Marianne, but she still clings far too much to the belief that they can keep this perfect, normal life forever. Will is still in the dark, thinking he has nothing but a superstitious wife who likes candles and incense a bit more than normal.

"Not yet," Marianne repeats. "She's too young. Soon, but not yet."

Then *soon* arrives, and we all know how that story ends.

GRACE DOESN'T MOVE.

She sat in silence through the whole sordid tale, her face betraying nothing as I told her of the parts we played in the deaths of her grandparents and later her parents.

Dean who she never met, but brought her grandmother back from the darkness.

Serafine who destroyed herself to buy a life for her daughter.

Will who died without ever knowing the truth of the women in his life.

And Marianne, stubborn, willful Marianne who just wanted to be free.

They weren't just her parents and her grandparents. They were *people*. Imperfect people that had dreams and made mistakes.

And all our lives have been entangled since long before Lucifer and Grace crossed paths in the square.

Grace takes a sharp breath inward and looks up at me, and I see Serafine in those eyes.

"I can't forgive you because there's nothing to forgive."

She reaches across the space between us and grasps my hand, never breaking my gaze. "There's nothing to forgive," she repeats.

Heaven doesn't want me, and if I'm truly being honest with myself, I've been an outcast for far longer than just today.

I can never go home. The gates are barred to me as much as they are to Lucifer and the other Fallen, but for the first time, I don't care.

Free will. Those two little words sent Lucifer to perdition and sent Serafine into a new life on the golden coast. They made Michael lay down his sword and gave Milly the drive to escape her abuser on a Greyhound bus. They made Elissa choose magic over powerlessness and let Phenex take that first step to follow Lucifer into the Pit.

Those two words let the Devil fall in love.

Nothing and everything has changed since last night, but I whisper those two words like a prayer, and I feel ready.

Let them come.

11

PHENEX

Something has shifted between us all.

While the tension outside twists tighter and tighter with each day and night that bleeds away, inside the two well-worn houses that have become our bases it fades into nothing.

Such close proximity and high nerves had us at each other's throats a few days ago. Michael and Lucifer sniped endlessly at each other as they both unconsciously vied for control, while Elissa, Caila, and Grace tiptoed around each other, trying to avoid the tangled mess of their shared history and the guilt and regret that came with it.

And then there's me. I'm still plagued with flashes of Brielle, of Lucifer. The sight of blood, the stink of demons, the feeling of flesh tearing beneath my blades – that's all it takes for the memories to come screaming to the forefront. I push past them, telling myself over and over and over that it's not real. That it's over.

Sometimes it even works. But not for long.

Caila's touch quiets it. I can still feel all my demons, literal and metaphoric, clawing at the edges, but when I feel her against me I can close my eyes without fearing the blackness.

The wave of chaos that coursed through the city at the first breach has quieted. The running tally of the body count certainly doesn't match up with the masses we saw escape the rift, so there can be no more doubt that someone is controlling them.

Now the only goal is to find out who.

IT DOESN'T MATTER what day of the week, Bourbon Street is always a party. While the slightly more sedate revelers keep to Royal and Dauphine Streets, enjoying the reverberation of drums and horns from the street performers while avoiding the stench of spilled beer and garbage and the crush of the crowds, Bourbon is still the place to go if you're searching for someone to share an anonymous night with.

Grace and Elissa weave through the crowds a few feet apart. Elissa clutches the same clear plastic cup in her hand as the rest of the crowd, the sticky sweet concoction of rum, fruit juice, and even more rum melting in her hand as she walks with a surprisingly convincing stagger. Even though she's still dressed in her usual black on black ensemble, the go cup and the pile of bright plastic beads around her neck makes her blend into the crowd.

Grace though? She's not there to blend in. She's bait.

Her fingers are wrapped around another cup, and when she turns too quickly the sticky drink sloshes over the side, coating her hand with the drink.

She giggles loudly, apologizing to no one as she weaves down the middle of the street. A pair of platform wedges dug up from the back of her closet add a few inches to her height, and the shorts she wears are skimpy enough to barely count as clothing even on Bourbon Street. The equally tiny white tank top she wears is almost totally hidden by strands of gold and green and purple beads that clack together as she moves.

Dozens of heads swivel as she passes, copious alcohol and the vacation mindset stripping away any chance at subtlety, but Grace is trying to catch a true hunter tonight.

I don't see Lucifer in the crowd, but I know he's close. Grace can take care of herself, but he still refuses to let her out of his sight when she's wobbling down the dirty streets and looking like prey. In the shadows of a side street or perched on a balcony Caila and Michael are ready as well.

And somewhere in this crowd that throbs and pulses like a living thing, an incubus is hunting.

Elissa notices it first. Her posture instantly goes rigid, the guise of an unconcerned coed on a summer bender dropping away. She tosses her cup into an overflowing trash barrel as she takes a step closer to the creature circling Grace.

Despite her appearance, Grace is far from oblivious. She catches my eye for an instant, nodding so imperceptibly that I would have missed the signal if I'd blinked. She takes another wobbly step forward and catches the toe of her shoe on the broken asphalt. She pitches forward, her plastic cup landing in the street in a splatter of cheap rum and corn syrup.

The incubus' arms curl around her waist, saving her from the same messy fate as her beverage, and Grace turns in its arms, fixing it with the wide-eyed stare that makes everyone underestimate her.

"My hero!" she giggles, biting her pink-lacquered lip as she gazes up at it through her eyelashes. The act is bordering on ridiculous, but it's still one of the more demure flirtations going on tonight.

The incubus isn't any more interested in long-term romance than the rest of the crowd. Packs of drunken carousers hungry for sex and debauchery make an all-night buffet for the incubus, and Grace is just the latest morsel it has set its eyes on.

This one has taken its time to assimilate into the mortal world. Its hair hangs in soft blond waves past slender shoulders. Skinny jeans and a white seersucker shirt turn a demon of lust into a harmless hipster. A human might blame the spark of Hellfire glowing in its amber eyes on the streetlamps or even color contacts, and that would be the last choice they'd make before the incubus bled them dry.

"Let me buy you another drink," it purrs, tightening its arm around Grace's waist. The creature's long fingers brush Grace's hair away from her face, its touch ready to ignite her senses with a flood of lust that would burn her from the inside out if she were just another human.

The incubus freezes when it touches her. Instead of the glazed look of hunger that it expects to see, Grace is completely unaffected.

"What are you?" it hisses.

Grace smiles, and the silly drunken act dissolves. The incubus takes a step backward and runs into Elissa who shoves it into the mouth of an alley where the creature crumples at Lucifer's feet.

"Answers," Lucifer snarls, grabbing the incubus by its throat and dragging it upward. "Now."

The incubus barely spares a glance at Lucifer, craning its neck to look back at Grace. "Where did you find that delicious morsel, Lucifer?" it asks. "She's enough to make any of us forget ourselves, isn't she? I bet she tastes like strawberries-" The incubus' words cut off in a choked wheeze as Lucifer slams it against the wall of the alley.

A pack of bridesmaids in hot pink shirts with BEIGNETS BOOZE & BESTIES emblazoned across their chests pause to gawk at the fight for a moment before a blonde in a crumpled white veil drags them away.

Lucifer's eyes are smoldering red, his rage barely held in check at the incubus' words. Elissa sidles up next to him. "Maybe I should try," she murmurs, her soft words drawing Lucifer's attention enough that he loosens his grip on the creature's throat. "I can be very persuasive."

"Names," Lucifer grinds out. "Names and I'll make it quick. Otherwise, I'll take my time. I know what happens to your kind when you starve."

The incubus blanches at that before regaining its cocky demeanor. "You know who," it says. "You've always known. Asmodeus. Abaddon. Malphas. Azazel. Belial. Astaroth." It pauses after each name to allow the words to sink in. "The gang's all here. And they like this world. So new and unspoiled like a ripe peach. Or should I say an apple?" The incubus laughs at its own cleverness.

"Where are they?"

The incubus' eyes widen when Michael comes into view, his sword dangling at his side like an extension of his arm. This is not the weary Michael who longs for peace.

This is the archangel. Heaven's most deadly weapon.

Only Heaven doesn't own him anymore.

The creature's eyes dart between Michael and Lucifer, the feigned cockiness forgotten in the utter shock of seeing Michael and Lucifer side by side. "They'll kill me," it stammers.

"Because we won't?" Michael replies, easing past Elissa and Grace to stand next to his brother.

Lucifer's grip tightens, but the incubus doesn't react. "Look around you," it murmurs. "This world is lost. They just don't know it yet."

Michael responds by slamming his sword through its shoulder, hard enough that the metal crumbles a few pieces of the brick wall behind it. The incubus writhes on the blade, the touch of Heaven-forged metal burning its unclean body like acid.

"Where are they?" he snarls.

"Where aren't they?" the incubus wheezes. "Azazel enjoys the cemeteries. Abaddon has been playing with the weak and the sick as always. Asmodeus always liked the whores, but there are so many to choose among in this place. This world was built for us."

Lucifer closes his eyes, looking almost pained for an instant until the mask slips back into place.

"We won't get anything more of use from you, will we?"

The incubus scrabbles at the wall when Lucifer takes a step back to draw his weapon. Its muscles tense as if preparing to run, but Michael's blade still has it pinned to the bricks like an insect. Lucifer cleaves the creature's head off with a single stroke, leaving a deep gouge in the worn wall behind it.

He pauses for a moment, staring at the mess of gore that was taunting us seconds ago without seeming to really see it. When he turns to face us, he's the general again, but I've known him long enough to see the cracks in his mask.

He's afraid.

For the world. For this strange little family that's sprung up out of loss and vendettas. Maybe even for himself.

It's been a long time since either of us felt like we had something to lose.

"Now we know," he says, glancing over his shoulder at the incubus' body slowly crumbling into ash. He pushes past us, ignoring the questions on Grace's lips to stalk through the crowd.

"Let him go," Michael murmurs when Grace moves to follow.

Caila's hand rests on my shoulder, the comforting weight

tethering me here when the memories of Hell's worst Fallen swirl around me.

"I'll go after him."

It takes me a moment to realize that the words came from my mouth.

"Phenex," Michael begins, but I cut him off with a shake of my head before following Lucifer's path down the packed street.

I CATCH up with him a few blocks later. The crowd has thinned out on the darkened side streets. Only locals venture off the well-lit paths of the Quarter, so the streets are vacant. Our only other companion leans against a doorway, not bothering to look up as we pass. His face is in shadows, but the red cherry of a cigarette glows in his hand, the fingers gnarled with age.

"Lucifer."

He stops but doesn't turn around.

"Lucifer," I repeat.

He turns slowly, his movements telegraphed as if trying to calm a terrified animal. I'm not surprised. There's always a buffer between us since I told him the truth – Michael's glowering presence or Grace's quiet concern.

He blames himself for something he didn't do, and it's poisoning us both.

Brielle is dead. She doesn't get to still win.

"I don't regret anything, Lucifer." His brow furrows a bit at the non-sequitur, but he says nothing. "Falling. Hell. Following you here. It all had to happen."

Lucifer chuckles at that. "The Phenex I know never put much stock in prophecies or fate."

"This isn't about fate," I counter. "This is the opposite of putting everything up to fate or Heaven. We've all cursed Father for making us feel like puppets made to dance for His divine amusement. It's easier that way. Having someone to blame."

I move closer to Lucifer, closing the last block separating us, and I wait for the same cold dread to douse me when I get too close.

It's still there, still coiled like a snake in the back of my mind, but I shove past it, putting one foot in front of the other until I'm standing in front of Lucifer.

"Free will, right?" There's no tremor in my voice, and I can feel the tense knot of my nerves slowly unraveling as I force past my fear to really *look* at Lucifer.

Brielle made a good copy, but it was still a copy. Those eyes that stared impassively down at me as I crouched on the cold stone were never his. The fists that shattered my bones were never his.

The Devil only punishes the wicked, after all.

What was I guilty of?

"The past is the past?" Lucifer asks. "It's all that easy?"

"You call this easy?"

Lucifer lets out a bark of laughter at that before tensing as though the sudden noise would send me into a tailspin.

"I didn't ask you to coddle me, Lucifer. I survived. Caila survived. You and Michael and Grace and Elissa survived that mansion. But if we let what happened rule the rest of our lives, why did we bother? It would have been a lot easier to lay down and let the blaze take us. Do you think Belial or Azazel or any of them will give a damn if we're battle ready or not?"

Lucifer quirks an eyebrow at that. "When did you become the voice of reason in our lives? I seem to recall your motto being more along the lines of Nero playing the fiddle while Rome burned."

"Things change."

"They certainly do."

Lucifer looks skyward, and I don't need to ask just who his cold gaze is directed at. He repeats my words softly, almost to himself, but this time it isn't a question.

"Free will."

12

CAILA

"If Hell had archangels, it would be those six, and they're here."

The atmosphere inside Grace's house is strained, the bright moments of the past few days forgotten under the pall of what we're up against.

Elissa sits perched on Grace's kitchen counter, tucked against the window underneath a fragrant bundle of rosemary drying in the sun. Her hands are busy in her lap, idly polishing one of her blades on the edge of her t-shirt.

Michael leans against the counter beside her. Elissa's knee bumps against his hip in an erratic rhythm, the nervous energy overflowing from her needing a physical outlet. Without speaking, Michael reaches back and covers her hand with his, stilling her movement on the knife.

Lucifer paces the length of the tight room as he speaks. "Everyone in this room needs to be aware of just what we're dealing with." He glances past me to where Phenex stands in the doorway. "Phenex and I are the only two that really understand what those six are capable of. Michael, Caila, you may have heard stories, but you don't know the truth." He turns to where Grace sits at the kitchen table, and his desire to shield her from all of this is carved into his face.

"You don't need to protect me from this," she says flatly. "I've seen it all, remember?"

I heard only the barest details from Elissa, but that spell nearly broke Grace, almost crushing her mind under the weight of Lucifer's long, painful history. Lucifer flinches at that reminder but he pushes on.

A few days ago we had the luxury of time. Time to process the jumble of regrets and mistakes that bound us all together. Time to heal and forgive.

That time is past.

Lucifer continues without missing a beat. "Asmodeus is the most straightforward of the six. He's lust made flesh. This isn't the lust of pop songs or pornography. This is the ugly, brutal side of desire that makes that incubus look like the type you'd bring home to meet your parents. He makes your own desires come to the surface, hidden things that shame you, and he twists them until they tear you apart." Lucifer pauses to stare at Grace before pushing on, and I wonder what shared memory is trying to claw its way to the surface.

"Abaddon is pestilence. Disease. The weakening of the flesh. She's been called the angel of death in some writings, but she is not a merciful passing. Her pleasure comes in the suffering and the decay. She's given life to plagues with all the joy of a proud mother."

"Malphas is the deceiver. His trade is artifice and betrayal. He'll be the one crouched behind the world leaders, whispering just how easy it would be to launch a missile and end their enemies."

"What happened to the Devil not controlling humans?" Grace asks. The question is innocent, but something flickers in Lucifer's eyes at her words.

His voice is clipped when he replies, every consonant

sharp. "We aren't speaking of my actions, and they aren't under my rule anymore." His voice softens, the weariness we all feel slipping into his tone and dulling the edge. "But even if they were, nothing they do is pulled from the ether. They twist the semantics how it suits them, they draw the seeds of darkness to the surface, but those seeds were still *there*."

Lucifer takes a step back from Grace to continue his story, but before he moves out of reach she catches his hand, squeezing it quickly before letting go. One corner of Lucifer's mouth raises up into a tiny half-smile at that before he continues on with his narrative as if that digression had never happened.

"Astaroth is the only one we might be able to reason with. She wasn't always one of mine, but her heart grew cruel when the mortals that once worshipped at her feet in Babylon twisted her name into something evil. Better to reign in Hell than be forgotten. She likes false piety. If there's a church with nasty secrets in this town, we'll find her there."

"Belial is chaos. The angel of lawlessness. He's the one who just wants to watch the world burn because he likes the color of the flames. Wherever he can cause the most havoc at once, that's where he'll be."

"And Azazel?"

Lucifer ducks his head. "Azazel. It was too much to hope for that she wouldn't make it out. She was there from the beginning, even before the Fall. I was the scapegoat, but she was the one who taught humanity the ways of war and violence. She slipped that rock into Cain's hand and whispered for him to do what the blackness of his soul desired because she wanted to see what would happen."

I remember Azazel. Even in the earliest days, she stood apart from us all. We didn't understand the darkness around her. Before the humans, there was no war, no death, no pain. We had no concept of suffering, yet corruption clung to her skin like some hidden scent causing even the archangels to keep their distance.

"We were all children in the dawn of the universe pulling the wings off insects because we knew no better. I just wanted the freedom to ask why or say no, but Azazel wanted to take apart our Father's new toys and see just what made them tick." Lucifer's voice trails off into silence. There's nothing else to say.

"We're in over our heads." Phenex's quiet voice cuts through the tense stillness in the room. "We might be able to handle a few of them but all six? They're still just toying with this world, trying to figure out what they want to do first. Once they figure it out. . ." His voice falters, and none of us push for him to continue. "We need help from anyone that's willing to give it."

Lucifer's pride fights a silent war across his face. Hell was his kingdom, after all. His domain. For all he despised it, for all that he wanted to leave and be free of the darkness he was imprisoned in, it was all he knew for so long.

For thousands of years, none of the Fallen would have dared challenge his rule. And then he walked away, chose that freedom he ached for over the shackles Heaven bound him in, and now he has to contend with the idea of begging Heaven for aid.

Prideful or not though, Lucifer is no fool.

"We don't have a lot of choices on that front," he mutters. "Raphael always was saner than most of that lot. He might be a possibility. Or Gabriel. Beyond that though, I don't know. The lower angels would fly away screaming at the sight of me, and the rest are under Metatron's thumb. Raphael or Gabriel are the only ones left who might even consider disobeying him."

I never shared the outcome of my brief trip to Heaven with anyone but Phenex. Speaking the story aloud turned the twisted nightmare of blood and death inside the quiet of Eden something that I couldn't forget.

So I kept silent, and Phenex told no one.

But I can't allow Michael to walk into Heaven unaware of what might be waiting for him.

"We won't be getting any help from Heaven." Five heads swivel to stare at me as I begin. After a moment, understanding softens Phenex's surprise. I doubt this is the last secret buried between us but I'm glad to share this burden instead of bearing it alone.

It's as though I'm reading from the pages of a book at first. My voice stays flat and modulated as I follow the trail through Eden, treading the paths Uriel walked alone in those days when he wasn't causing havoc on Earth. I can almost smell the flowers in the air and the warm scent of the soil beneath my feet, and it's easy to be lulled back into that serenity.

But just as I couldn't stay in the quiet of the Garden, I can't linger there now. I try not to hear the quaver in my voice when I come across Sariel.

You're no better than the Fallen.

You are worse *than the Fallen.*

I don't feel the tears on my cheeks when I leave him for dead, his blood soaking into the green grass.

I don't look up. The silence in the room is thick as old blood, and I don't want to see Elissa's anger or Grace's sadness yet. When I finally drag my eyes upwards, it's Michael's soft blue stare that meets mine first.

He looks resigned. None of this surprises him in the slightest.

But there's still a spark of hope underneath it all.

"I still have to try. No one has seen Gabriel in so long that I wouldn't even know where to begin the search." One less hope. One less potential betrayal. "Raphael has always been reasonable," Michael continues. "He wants peace in both our worlds." Michael sighs deeply and takes a step away from Elissa, already mentally readying himself for the meeting.

"After hearing what happened to you, there's no way I can risk returning to Heaven alone. Caila, you were lucky that you weren't seen by anyone but Sariel, and I don't trust that luck to hold a second time."

Elissa speaks up. "We can summon him. Somewhere neutral so we won't need to take down the wards."

Michael nods. "I need to do this alone."

"No."

Lucifer's voice is little more than a growl, and he leaves no opening for any discussion.

Of course, Michael has to protest. He and Lucifer are still far too alike to keep from clashing at every turn. "How many millennia has it been since you've spoken with Raphael, brother? Do you think he's more likely to believe you than me?"

Lucifer strides forward until he's nose to nose with Michael. "This lone wolf bullshit doesn't fucking work," he snarls. "Is everyone in this room aware of how lucky we are that no one has ended up dead yet? We are all at the top of both Heaven and Hell's hit lists." His eyes dart across the room, his black gaze pausing on each one of us, forcing us all to remember every instance where we ran off half-cocked and only survived out of sheer luck. "The only people we can depend on are in this room. So no brother, I'm not letting you jaunt off to see Raphael alone."

Lucifer takes a step back from Michael but six inches of breathing room does nothing to decrease the pressure. "Raphael may be the most reasonable one left, but he still belongs to Heaven. His loyalty is to *Heaven*, not you." Lucifer's voice lowers, the anger draining from him, leaving behind a very real fear that he makes no effort to conceal. "I don't want this to be the one time Metatron decides to get his hands dirty, and you're by yourself."

Michael nods in defeat, any thoughts of continuing to protest lost in the face of Lucifer's argument.

After all, this wouldn't be the first time Heaven threatened to make an example of him.

One day, those words will stop being threats.

When that day comes, I think the first war will pale.

13

PHENEX

The Celestin tomb looms ahead of us. In the waning moonlight, the snow-white marble looks grey as dead flesh. Elissa cups a bright orange flame in her palm, the light illuminating the deeper shadows next to the mausoleum. She scrawls the angular sigil that will summon Raphael onto the marble, her eyes narrowed with concentration.

A few feet away, Lucifer sits on the edge of a smaller tomb, his fingers drumming against the marble as he waits. Beside him, Grace watches Elissa's movements with an absent look that tells me her mind is somewhere else entirely.

It's not hard to guess where.

After leaving an indignant Grace behind in his room at The Saint, Lucifer's plan had been for the two of us to search for the streets for Michael. We'd barely made it a block down the street when that iron coin with Lucifer's sigil that Grace carried like a lucky charm told him she was on the move. We trailed her to the cemetery before Lucifer sent me away.

Better to not let Michael know you're here just yet.

You'll know if I need you.

The next time I saw the Last, she was as she is now. Those last scraps of mortality that held her back crumbled into ash.

Here. She woke up here, surrounded by the bones of her family.

I might have missed the fireworks, but Grace has been surprisingly willing to fill in the blanks. It wasn't easy. It wasn't quick, and it wasn't painless. She nearly broke that night. Nearly lost everything that made her who she is as she drowned under the might of Heaven filling her body.

Then Lucifer upended both of their worlds.

It's hard to believe how little time has passed since that day. At least on Earth, it's barely been two months, but those days feel like another life entirely.

Caila and Michael stand a few feet away from Elissa in the middle of one of the many worn gravel paths that crisscross between the graves. Michael's back is ramrod straight, his posture stiff. His eyes never stray from Elissa. He once trusted Raphael. He once trusted Heaven. And now all he's left with is this motley band we've patched together. I search his face for regrets, but I don't see a single one.

And Caila. My Caila. I never expected her. Never expected anything in my life beyond the long, unbroken chain of hedonism for its own sake. No one but Lucifer ever mattered. All the rest were just bodies. Just *entertainment*. Just distractions from my perpetual quest for more.

Caila shifts on her feet, that angelic grace lost in apprehension as she waits.

Neither she nor Michael can get used to thinking of Heaven as an enemy.

I wish they didn't have to.

Elissa purses her lips and blows out the flame in her palm. A wisp of smoke curls toward the sigil, the lines glowing orange for a moment before fading back to grey.

"It's done," she says. "He'll come or he won't, but he knows we called."

Elissa wanders over to my side, leaning against another ornately carved tomb. She glances back at Michael. Already mentally preparing for a battle he doesn't want any part of, Michael doesn't notice.

"It'll be all right."

Elissa chuckles darkly at my meaningless platitude. "Sure it will. We'll all live happily ever after."

I can't exactly fault her cynicism. I reach into the depths of yet another borrowed suit jacket. My fingers find the hidden pocket, closing around the smooth metal flask I stashed there earlier.

That brings a genuine laugh from Elissa as she unscrews the lid and takes a swallow of the whiskey. She doesn't blink at the burn. "You angels always come prepared, don't you?"

"Always."

We collectively hold our breath until the sound of wing beats cutting through the quiet night alerts us to Raphael's arrival.

Raphael doesn't attempt to hide his shock when he lands. His brown eyes stay wide as his head swivels between Michael and Caila to Lucifer and Grace. The black of his pupils nearly swallows up the warm wood of his eyes in the low light of the cemetery.

Nearly all the angels in Heaven would be more than terrified to find themselves summoned into Lucifer's presence, but for all his obvious surprise, Raphael keeps his cool.

He has always been the healer. It was who picked up the pieces after the war in Heaven and all the myriad of wars on Earth. If Raphael can't bring himself to care of the havoc that will come to Earth with those six on the loose, no one else will.

A breeze picks up, flapping the length of the tan trenchcoat he wears like a second set of wings. No angel is ever unarmed, but he keeps his hands in view as he steps closer to us.

He tilts his head at Michael, acknowledging his presence, but his focus never drifts from Lucifer.

"Hello, brother."

Lucifer smirks at that. No one in Heaven has called him brother for millennia. Even Michael stumbles over the word on occasion, their reunion still so fresh that old habits still cling to his voice.

That word is no accident, and I feel the tiniest spark of hope.

Then Raphael registers just who the woman sitting next to Lucifer is. "The Last," slips from his mouth and Lucifer's entire demeanor changes in a blink. The temperature plummets around us, the balmy night growing cold as thunder growls in the distance, nature itself growing threatening at Raphael's innocent words.

Lucifer stands up, taking a menacing step forward. I'm impressed that Raphael holds his ground.

"We called you here for a reason, Raphael, and it has nothing to do with Grace."

Michael quiet voice snaps Lucifer back to the task at hand. I think we're all a bit shocked to watch him defer to Michael without quarrel, but Raphael and Lucifer are as good as strangers after so much time.

"Six of the most powerful Fallen have breached Hell's borders," Michael begins. The gravel crunches beneath his boots as he circles Raphael to stand beside Lucifer.

His choice of position isn't lost on any of us.

"We don't know their plans beyond the obvious chaos and death. We've been doing nothing but reacting, killing soldier demons that crawled out with them while they've had nothing but time to grow stronger." Michael doesn't blink as he stares at Raphael, well aware that all of Heaven knows the side he chose.

"We need help or this world will fall."

"And what's to stop them from clawing their way to the gates once they've finished with Earth?" Lucifer adds.

Raphael says nothing. It's been too many years to count since the last time I crossed paths with the bookish archangel. Like us all, he wielded his sword when pressed into action, but he never excelled at battle and bloodshed.

While Uriel stayed wrapped in his robes and snarled in the past until it destroyed him, refusing even the smallest changes, Raphael has adapted to this modern world with a familiar ease. A tan trenchcoat hides his more slight frame, so different than the intimidating bulk of Michael or the compact, predatory stature of Lucifer.

His dark hair is shorn close to the coffee-colored skin of his skull, even shorter than Michael's. The breeze pushes his coat open again, exposing the smoke grey suit underneath. He wouldn't look out of place behind a podium, speaking to a class of eager young minds of the ways to heal the world.

"Heaven is aware."

With those three worlds, the bookish demeanor surrounding Raphael drops away. Disgust and loyalty war across his face for an instant before he forces himself back into quiet neutrality.

"Heaven is aware," he repeats. "And it wants no part."

He scrubs his hand across his face, a gesture so human that I know without a doubt that Raphael has been taking his own leave from Heaven's ivory towers. He sucks in a breath as if bracing himself for our reaction to his next words.

"'If the Morningstar cares so much for humanity, let him be the one to save it,'" he parrots.

"Those are Metatron's words, not yours," Lucifer hisses. "You're an archangel. The only archangel Heaven has left.

And you're going to let our Father's secretary put words in your mouth?"

"Our Father isn't here," Raphael snaps back. "And I am the only archangel now." He looks pointedly at Michael, but he fails to rise to the bait.

"You're doing nothing?" Caila's clear voice echoes across the cemetery, louder than she intended, but the prospect of leaving this meeting with nothing has us all dangerously close to hysteria. "You're just going let this world burn? His world?"

Raphael bows his head before answering. "Caila. My orders are to execute you on sight."

Five sets of hands have their weapons at the ready before Raphael can blink. Elissa circles behind Raphael, her feet no more than a whisper on the gravel as she travels to where Caila stands alone. She meets Raphael's cool gaze without blinking, saying without any words how quickly she'll end him if it comes to that.

Raphael raises both hands in surrender. "I have no intentions of following through with that order or any other," he says.

"Any other?" Elissa demands, her grip still unwavering on her dagger.

"Each one of you is to be executed. Decreed by Metatron himself." Raphael sighs, and for the first time, I pity him. "I have no plans to raise my sword against any of you, but my hands are tied. You'll receive no aid from Heaven. Metatron's power grows each day, and I can't risk being ousted myself. I won't leave Heaven to his whims."

He takes a step closer to where Michael and Lucifer stand. Nearly in unison, they sheath their weapons.

The bond between the archangels goes far deeper than what the rest of the host of Heaven shares. The first beings created when the world was young and the first to know our Father's love and wrath, they always kept to themselves.

Lucifer was the first to abandon his place at the top of the angelic food chain to pass time with the rest of us rabble, but long before I could call myself his right hand, he was Michael's and Michael was his.

Uriel was the only one who preferred his own company to that of his siblings, and it was Raphael and Gabriel who were thick as thieves. No wonder Raphael looks so off balance.

"I don't begrudge you for the choice you made, Michael." Raphael grasps his brother's hand for a moment before releasing him and taking a few steps back from them both, putting distance between himself and the brothers Heaven told him to despise. "But I can't take the chance. With you gone, I'm the only archangel left."

"What about Gabriel?" Michael asks.

Raphael shakes his head. "Why would Gabriel return now of all times? I'm sorry, brother."

"So that's it then?" I mutter. Raphael turns to me. Once, I would have held my tongue around another archangel. I had Lucifer's loyalty, but self-preservation always seemed the better option over bravado.

Apparently, my survival instinct has left the building.

"We'll get no help from Heaven, so what now? Pour a stiff drink and wait for the apocalypse? Smoke them if you've got them?" The darkness crawls at the edge of my vision as the flashbacks try to fight their way to the forefront, but I gulp down the humid night air. The heat crept back once Lucifer's spark of misplaced rage was extinguished, and the warmth calms me.

It's so different than the damp, stale air of Hell.

"I'm not going back," I say vehemently. "None of us are. Ever."

"Phenex, that almost hurts my feelings."

No. Not her. Not now when we're all so woefully unprepared.

She emerges from between two tombs a few feet from where Raphael stands. The shadows cling to her as if she's made from them.

Maybe she was. Of all the creatures in Heaven and Hell, she's truly unique. A being without mercy, without love. A husk that walks and talks and kills for no other reason than curiosity.

Perhaps that makes her more like our Father than any of us. He made us all from nothing simply because He could. And she'll unmake us for the same reason.

"Hello, Azazel."

"Phenex," she purrs. "What company you keep now." Her dark eyes flit from Lucifer to Michael to Raphael before finally settling back onto me. "You did always have a thing for archangels, but it's bordering on a fetish at this point."

Azazel looks utterly unconcerned at the crowd. I scan the surrounding tombs, searching for any hint of movement that would betray more of her cohorts waiting to ambush us and see nothing. She's alone.

She still looks just as she did in Hell, clad in the same leather armor that hugs her frame like a second skin as she flips the sheet of glossy black hair over her shoulder. The sheer anachronism of it should look ridiculous, but all I can think of is the joy across her gore-spattered face as she dismantled a corrupt soul bit by bit.

One I watched her remove a man's spine and show it to him, one vertebra at a time. She made him count, and once he reached 33, she started anew.

She ran through it three times before he broke.

Lucifer steps around Raphael and Michael until he's within striking distance, and I want to scream for him to back up. Even in the depths of Hell, even in those first days when we wallowed in the darkness beside them, something about Azazel made my skin crawl.

"You don't belong here."

"Neither do you," she spits. Her eyes slither over Elissa and Caila before coming to rest on Grace. "We follow you into Hell, and then you abandon us to play house with a *human?*"

"You never followed anyone, Azazel," Lucifer shoots back, drawing her attention back to him.

It works far too well. Azazel sidles forward, pressing the length of her lithe body against Lucifer. "Does she know all the things you've done?" she asks in a stage whisper. "You weren't always such a *good boy*, were you?"

Lucifer shoves her away, and she starts laughing, and there's not a damned soul in Hell that doesn't remember that laugh. It cuts off as abruptly as it began when her attention snaps back to Grace.

"You left us. I didn't mind at first. When the cat's away, after all. But things got boring, and then suddenly there were doors." Azazel smirks. "They were locked at first, but the locks weren't made to last long. I think whoever made those doors wanted to let us out to play."

"Hell wasn't enough for you?"

Lucifer's question incenses Azazel, and the taunting banter turns on a dime. She grabs the front of Lucifer's jacket, hauling him closer. "Was it enough for you?" she whispers, close enough to kiss. "You said it yourself. We couldn't corrupt a pure soul if we tried. None of them are pure." She lets go, dancing away from Lucifer before he can draw a weapon. "Corrupt and vicious and unbearably stupid, the whole lot of His perfect little creations. They *all* belong to Hell. There is no such thing as a pure soul."

"You know that's not what I meant."

"Is it? Sin is sin. Evil is evil. You're going to argue degrees with me, Lucifer?"

"You were an angel once, or have you forgotten?"

"I remember," she replies coolly, fixing Raphael with an icy stare. "We all remember Heaven. You seem to be the one who forgot where he came from."

In my peripheral vision, I see Michael slowly creeping closer, trying to flank her, but that would be all too easy. Azazel pivots before Michael can strike and tosses him against a mausoleum with a flick of her wrist. The blow barely dazes him, and he's back on his feet an instant later.

Azazel is many things, but she's not stupid and while her power might rival an archangel, she's not foolish enough to take on three at once.

She rests two fingers against her forehead before flicking them at Lucifer in a mock salute as she melts back into the darkness.

"Be seeing you very soon."

⚝ 14 ⚝
CAILA

The book lands on the scarred wood of the desk with a heavy thud, shattering the uncomfortable silence.

Elissa tossing another spellbook to one of us is nothing new. From the most mainstream spellbooks that the nouveau witches of the 21st century are pumping out because even the arcane arts can be monetized to the most esoteric tomes with faded words in long dead languages written on cracked parchment, we've searched them all for answers. And just as Lucifer and Michael's hunts have come up empty, so have those pages.

This one feels different. From the first look, it's unassuming. This is no horror movie reject bound in human skin. Once it was someone's pride. The gilt edges of the pages are scorched, but the worst of the damage has gone to the cover. The deep claret of the leather has bubbled and split near the edges, and a few charred pieces flake off to land on the surface of the desk. The spine has split, but the stitching still holds, binding the pages with the blackened cover. The scent of fire rises from it almost as if the pages are still smoldering.

Elissa pushes it toward me, her fingers leaving streaks in

the thin coat of ash coating the cover. She touches it as little as possible, moving the book with only the tips of her fingers as if she's touching something vile.

I look up, a question in my eyes. Whatever this is, it certainly isn't something she picked up in the bontanicas she frequents.

"It's Brielle's. I went back."

My stomach twists at the mention of her name, but it's not fear that keeps me from touching the book. I don't expect Brielle to rise from the pages when I flip open the cover like some B-movie monster. There's a reason Elissa kept this hidden from us for so long, and it's nothing good.

Elissa's face tells the entire story.

A yellow post-it note pokes out between the pages near the end of the book, the bright paper looking more than a little ridiculous against the singed pages.

"You had this all along?" Lucifer's voice is clipped as he snatches the book from between us, flipping it open to the marked page. The post-it flutters to the ground.

"You'll see why," Elissa replies, her voice dull as she sinks down into one of the overstuffed chairs. "I thought about burning it for good this time. I wish I hadn't found it, but I did." Her fingers dig into cushions of the chair, and I've seen that fidget far too often not to recognize the way Elissa gets when there's nothing she can fix and no one she can fight.

I peer over Lucifer's shoulder to get a look at the page that's important enough to mark. The elegant scrip flows across the page, the French text studded with whorls and delicate ornamentation. Under the ash and grime, the book is well made, the thick linen paper strong enough to have survived centuries. It's just the sort of ostentation Brielle would demand from even a simple book.

It barely takes a page for me to realize that this *isn't* just another spellbook from Brielle's private collection. These are *her* spells written in her own hand.

I hear Lucifer's breath catch and I look away from the pages to see his face fall abruptly. Before I can read any further, he snaps it shut, causing a few more motes of ash and dust to fall to the floor.

"Another sacrifice then?" he growls, dropping the book back onto the desk as if he can't bring himself to touch it for longer than necessary. The sound in his voice isn't the blinding rage the incubus pulled from him or even the cold fury Azazel managed to summon.

It's weariness. Loss. Regret.

He isn't looking at me or Elissa or even Grace.

I follow his gaze and see that he's staring at Phenex.

Out of the corner of my eye, I notice Grace go pale at the word *sacrifice*. Erzulie's prophecy almost cost her everything but they survived in the end. They *won*.

Elissa kills that hope before it can begin to take root. "Another sacrifice," she repeats. "And this isn't some ancient prophecy where you can wiggle out on semantics. This is exactly what she did to open those rifts, and it's exactly what we'll have to do to close them."

I stare at Elissa, and everything clicks into place. The lack of sleep, the obsessive searching, the furtive, guilty gazes she casts me — they finally make sense. She knew, and she was trying to find another way.

Not Phenex. Please not him.

"What sacrifice?"

Phenex's voice is quiet, but I don't miss the tiny tremor in his voice. He sounds like he already knows what's coming, like he's trying and failing to resign himself to his fate.

Elissa presses her hand against the top of the book. The tendons in her hand twitch at the contact, her senses wanting to yank it back like a child touching a hot stove. She keeps her hand still. "It takes blood, of course," she begins. "A lot of blood. From the spellcaster and from an angel."

"I'll do it." Michael doesn't hesitate to throw himself on the sword. Always the warrior, ready to sacrifice himself for whatever cause he's shackled himself to.

Elissa smiles sadly but shakes her head. "It can't be you, Michael. Or you, Lucifer. You've never been to Hell, and Lucifer's Fallen." Elissa looks down at the burned leather of the cover peeking between her fingers.

She looks beyond broken, weeks of exhaustion leaving bruise-colored shadows that never fade under her eyes. She's given up the pretense of even attempting to sleep this past week, and now I know why. Nightmares don't always disappear when you open your eyes.

Please don't send him back there.

Elissa has never been a coward though. She forces herself to look up and meet my eyes as she finishes her explanation. "Phenex's blood opened the door, and only Caila's can close it. And it has to be done from the inside."

My ears ring as my suddenly sluggish mind tries to catch up with what Elissa just said.

Not Phenex.

Me.

"No." Phenex explodes, shaking his head wildly as if sheer vehemence would change the outcome. "There has to be another way."

"Do you think I haven't been searching for one?" Elissa snaps. "Do you think I want to put her through that again?" She deflates, the strength that flare of anger gave her dissipating as quickly as it came. "There's no other way. I can slap patches on the rifts as we find them, but we all know they won't hold for long. Azazel and the rest of them made it through already, and you know as well as I do that they're just the start. The world's a big place, and we can't be everywhere at once. Every demon, every damned soul, every other Fallen. Hell, even the fucking Horsemen will end up here."

Elissa finally lets go of the book, backing away from the desk until she bumps into Michael. She stands still as he slides his arms around her. She doesn't react to the embrace at first, pushing him away as if unworthy of comfort. That stoic façade doesn't last for long until the stress and guilt and fear she's been drowning in finally comes to a crest. She buries her face in his chest, and we all try to ignore the shudders across her frame.

When Elissa speaks again, her voice is muffled. "If we don't stop this, it'll be the end of everything."

"I'll do it."

I wait for the detachment to come. When I slipped that blade between Sariel's ribs or when Brielle first took the whip to my back – it was easy to drift away and watch my actions like an outsider.

That doesn't happen this time.

"I'll do it," I repeat. I think of Serafine and Marianne and their short, mortal lives and how they fought so hard for survival.

The least I can do is follow in their footsteps.

No one else protests after Phenex's outburst. No one begs for another way. No one tries to stop me.

I'm glad of that. Screaming and railing against my fate won't do anything but make it more difficult.

I don't look at Phenex.

Elissa quickly extricates herself from Michael's arms. She pauses in the mouth of the hallway. "We can wait if you need more time," she offers.

For a moment I picture myself slipping into my bedroom with Phenex for a tearful goodbye, but I shake my head.

Let us keep that one perfect memory.

Elissa nods tightly before hurrying down the hallway to gather supplies.

Once Elissa leaves the atmosphere in the room is subdued. I keep my gaze focused down the hallway as I wait for her return. I don't want to see anyone's reaction. I'm so intent on the empty space of the doorway that I jump when Phenex touches me.

His arms wrap around my waist from behind, tight enough that my ribs would be protesting if I were mortal. He says nothing. He doesn't tell me that I don't have to do this or beg me to make another choice. He doesn't ask me to look at him or bury me under declarations of love.

He just tucks my head underneath his chin and holds me close, lulling me into calm with the sound of his breath.

There's nothing else we can do, and I won't doom the world to save myself. I'm not that selfish.

All too soon, Elissa emerges from her bedroom clutching the supplies she needs – a container of salt, a bronze bowl, and a rough marble mortar and pestle filled with herbs. A thick black marker rolls around in the bowl. Everything you need to close a doorway to Hell.

Well, that and my blood.

Elissa waits until I step out of the circle of Phenex's arms, tilting my head toward her as if to say *I'm ready*.

I don't trust my voice.

Elissa thrusts the mortar and pestle into Grace's hands. "Grind those," she orders, dumping the rest of her supplies on the desk before shoving one of the armchairs over, clearing a large space on the floor.

She grabs the salt, the bright blue package looking so mundane and out of place that it's almost funny. She pours a thick layer on the floor as she walks slowly in a circle.

When she's finished the protective circle is nearly six feet in diameter, more than enough space to hold two people.

"This is to bind the spell," Elissa says, answering our questions before any of us muster the courage to ask. "As long as this circle isn't broken, nothing can make it out. It's an insurance policy in case I screw this up."

With the circle finished, Elissa grabs the marker and begins scrawling the angular symbols across the floor. The rhythmic scraping as Grace grinds the herbs pauses as she notices the odd juxtaposition of a Sharpie being used in an ancient spell.

Elissa notices Grace's scrutiny and shrugs. "The blood will activate these no matter what I draw them in. Ashes would be more traditional, but the last thing we need is one of these smearing and letting something else out. The circle might keep it from escaping, but I'll still be inside that circle."

Elissa clicks the cap back onto the marker and tosses it aside, squinting at the markings. Once she's satisfied that there are no mistakes she gets to her feet with the words, "Guess we'll be refinishing the floors if we don't all die."

No one laughs.

Elissa takes the mortar from Grace without another word and pours the contents into a carved bronze bowl before turning to me. "Are you ready?"

"Wait."

It's Lucifer that stops us. He flips the book open, paging through it frantically to find the correct passage. He scrutinizes the page one last time, searching for something, anything that Elissa might have missed.

I'm not surprised when he slams it shut a minute later.

He steps between Elissa and me, and the Devil grips my hand, demanding that I meet his gaze. "You don't belong to Hell," he states. "*Remember that.* Hell cannot keep you. We *will* get you out."

The intensity in his eyes makes me almost believe him.

"We need to do this now, Lucifer. Before it gets worse." I

let Elissa lead me to the edge of the circle. We both delicately step across the salt line, careful to not disturb a single grain. In unison, we kneel. Elissa places the bowl between us, the bronze clanging softly against the wood. She leans across it until I can feel her breath on my ear.

These words are only for me.

"Listen to me, Caila." She keeps her voice low, and the rest of the room probably thinks it's nothing but a tearful goodbye. "Once it opens, you can't hesitate. I can hold the rift open for a minute or so, but that's it. Any longer and I risk losing control of it, and then we have a new problem."

Her voice trails off, and I almost pull away until her fingers tighten on my wrist. "When you're inside, you'll know what to do, but I can't promise that closing these gates won't kill you." Elissa's voice cracks, but she doesn't stop. "I didn't write this spell, but Brielle wasn't exactly concerned with your welfare. It's going to hurt, and it's not going to be quick."

"It's okay." I don't know if my words are directed to Elissa or myself, but for now, it's enough.

Elissa sits back on her heels, making no effort to conceal the stricken look on her face from me. She holds her hand over the bronze bowl and opens her mouth to speak the word that will ignite its contents and start the spell.

"Thank you," I whisper. I don't elaborate, but after sixty years of friendship, I don't need to.

Elissa's jaw tightens, but she doesn't blink when she says, "Ignite."

The herbs burst into flames, the bitter, dry scent filling our lungs. The smoke rises around us but never crosses the barrier of the salt. It forms a hazy screen, blocking the world outside the circle from view.

Elissa slides the Hell-forged dagger from the sheath tucked at the small of her back. She presses the tip of the blackened blade just below her wrist, careful to avoid any major veins and slices the skin down to the crook of her elbow. Her flesh parts easily under the razor-sharp blade.

Blood wells up quickly from the deep cut, and the thick smell of copper joins the scent of smoke and burning herbs around us. Elissa presses her hand against the wound until her skin is stained red and the blood drips from between her fingers. She slams her palm on the ground, and the sound I hear isn't the faint slap of flesh on wood. It's the Earth cracking open to spew darkness into the world. It's the hollow noise of weapons clashing.

It's the *click click click* of heels on a stone floor.

The sigils peppering the floor around us stop being simple ink scribbled on worn wood. The shimmer like an oil slick, oozing along the floorboards like old blood, pulsing and moving like a living thing.

The blood still streams from Elissa's arm, but she doesn't look at the deep red rivulets flowing downward to pool on the floor beside her. She closed her eyes somewhere after that first cut, and when she opens them again they're pitch black, the whites and irises swallowed up by the darkness she's calling.

"Open."

The echo of the last syllable is still sounding when a slice appears in the air between us, raw and red as a fresh wound. It's far smaller than the rift in the alley, barely four feet tall, but it throbs like an artery.

Elissa rises slowly, and I mimic her movements. She reaches around the rift, careful not to touch the glowing red edges and presses the knife into my hand. The metal is sticky with her blood, and I clench it tightly.

"Remember what I told you," she breathes, those dead black eyes focused on me.

I say nothing as I take the first step through the portal.

🕊 15 🕊

PHENEX

She's gone.

The veil of smoke hid much of what went on within the circle from me. When the rift appeared, the bright red of it sliced through the haze, glowing in the air like an infected wound. I watched helpless as Caila rose to her feet and moved toward it. I wanted to scream for her to stop, that we'd find another way, but my voice died in my throat because she was right.

There was no other way.

Brielle made sure of that. From the beginning, she sealed both our fates. Even if we made it out of Hell, even if she *died*, she made certain that we would never really escape her.

Heaven did that to her. Twisted her love into cruelty and malice. I spare a glance at Lucifer, and he's not looking at Caila. His entire attention is focused on Grace. I look at him, but I see Brielle.

I don't want to think of what Lucifer will do if Grace is ever taken from him.

Seconds tick away. Caila doesn't look at Elissa or me or anywhere but forward. She ducks her head and steps through the opening. She doesn't falter. An instant later it seals up behind her as if the rift had never existed.

Trapping her back there. Alone.

My rational mind says that she's an angel. Our kind are not weak. We are made to endure, to survive centuries upon centuries as warriors for Heaven. We are not made to crumble.

But this is Hell. And she's alone.

"Bring her back." The desperate demand tumbles out of me, even though I know the futility of what I ask.

Elissa doesn't acknowledge me. She sways on her feet, her eyes still firmly shut as she rides the waves of the spell. The haze filling the circle begins to clear, the grey smoke fading as the fire at her feet dies out.

"Bring her back," I repeat, stepping closer to the thick mound of salt surrounding her.

Elissa's eyes fly open at my movement. They're still pure black, the pupils and whites swallowed up by the spell. It's impossible to know just where she's looking, but I have no doubt that her inky glare is fixed on me. "Back away," she growls, her voice cold, and I automatically take a step backward.

Underneath it all, she's still the same Elissa, but caught in the throes of this spell and roped to the Pit, she's something different. Something *familiar* in a way that makes my skin crawl.

"I'm the only thing tethering her here," Elissa says, her voice a low monotone. "I barely have her by a thread, but I can still feel her. You break this circle, I lose that." That unblinking black gaze bores into me and I realize just what that horrifying familiarity pouring off of her is.

Hell.

"You and Lucifer might have been able to find a way out in the past, but you know she won't. If she's lucky, she'll wander the plains of the damned until she goes mad. If she's not, something else will find her."

"Stop."

Elissa shivers, and her expression softens the tiniest amount as she tamps down the darkness that's scratching for control. She takes a slow breath, her eyes slipping closed again as she centers herself.

"Let me do this, Phenex. Let her do this."

I take another step back from the circle, but I still can't look away.

The tinny beeping of a cell phone cuts through the fog around me. I turn away from Elissa's still figure to see Grace fumbling with her phone, dread written across her face.

What now?

"Talia?"

The name means nothing to me, but it catches Lucifer's attention. He touches Grace's shoulder, trying to draw her notice. It doesn't work. Grace's entire focus is on the voice on the other end of the phone. The color drains from her cheeks at whatever she's hearing

"Talia," she interrupts. "I have someone here that can help. I'm going to put you on speaker."

She stabs the phone screen, her fingernail clicking against the glass, and a moment later a hushed voice pours out of the tiny speakers. "-know who else to call. You were in the middle of all that weird shit that went down last month, weren't you?" Talia doesn't wait for an answer. "You have to find him. Andre started his practicals at the hospital this week, and he called me and said there were these *things* overrunning the hospital."

Grace finally looks at Lucifer and mouths "*Demons?*"

"He was scared, Grace. I've never heard him like that. And then the line just went dead. I can't reach him, and no one's picking up any of the lines at the hospital." She keeps her voice low but there's no masking her fear.

"Are you and Sasha safe?"

"Yeah. Yeah, we are. She's coloring." Talia starts laughing, her voice taking on a hysterical edge before she reins it back in. "I'm hiding in the bathroom so she doesn't see me like this."

Grace presses her lips together before speaking, and I wonder what history the Last has with this woman. Lucifer takes the phone from Grace's hand. "Talia, do you remember me?"

Her breath catches, and when she speaks the quaver in her voice has steadied. "Lucifer."

"Yes, Lucifer." It's easy to forget the way most humans see Lucifer. He can pluck their darkest sins from their minds, dragging their transgressions forward. I've watched murderers drop to their knees in front of him and weep for their mothers and I've watched priests beg for the pleasure to serve him in any way he desires.

But those good, untainted souls? They're afraid. Millennia of bad PR will do that.

Not this Talia though, and I suspect Grace has more than a little to do with that.

"Do not leave your home for any reason. Do not open your door for anyone but Grace or myself." The authority in Lucifer's voice leaves no room for argument.

"What's happening?" Talia's words are barely above a whisper, as if she doesn't really want to know the answer.

Lucifer ignores her question. "We'll bring him back to you."

Grace takes her phone back and ends the call before turning to Lucifer. "He's at University Medical Center."

"If it's a hospital, then it's Abaddon," Lucifer finishes.

Michael glances at Elissa. Nothing has changed inside the circle. "Just Abaddon?" he asks.

Lucifer is already on the move, ready to put an end to at least one enemy tonight. "Yes," he answers. "In Hell, they tolerate each other, nothing more. One or more of them might tag along out of curiosity, but none of them will risk their neck for the other. There's no loyalty in Hell."

"Go." Elissa's quiet voice cuts through the room. She doesn't open her eyes or make any attempt to move from where she stands, just off center in the circle. "There's nothing else you can do here." Lucifer and Grace are already at the door with Michael a step behind. I hesitate, still staring at the space in the air Caila disappeared through.

The lightbulb above the kitchen sink shatters sending sparks and shards of glass down onto the countertop. Elissa opens her eyes and the voice that comes out of her is an inhuman snarl, "Go!"

THE HOSPITAL LOOKS like the aftermath of a war.

An ambulance sits in front of the entrance, the open back door swaying in the wind while the engine idles. The shrill whine of a heart monitor echoes out of the empty vehicle.

"Where is everyone?" Grace asks, peering inside as if she expects the paramedics to be hiding just out of view.

None of us answer. We all have our own guesses and none of them are good.

The heavy plate glass windows surrounding the entrance are shattered, blanketing the path in a thick layer of safety glass that crunches like ice beneath our feet. The air reeks of metal and the acrid scent of scorched electrical wires. And underneath it all, the stench of sulfur and rot.

I notice the blood first.

Nearly all of the lights in the main entryway are broken, the cracked fluorescent bulbs sending a few errant sparks raining down. The few that still work flicker erratically until one stays lit long enough to illuminate the diffused red spatter decorating the back wall.

No bodies, just blood.

Not just Abaddon then.

Abaddon learned her subtle trade at Pestilence's knee. While the Horseman was content with dispersing his plagues as widely as possible, spreading disease across the air and water like grains of pollen in spring, Abaddon was different.

In her eyes, epidemics were science and art rolled into one. She tended her diseases like flowers, testing them on souls and watching the inevitable decay like a play for her amusement.

Time flows faster in Hell, and a virus that would take days or weeks to fester and grow would take minutes or hours in Hell. She'd watch, reveling in the decay as the corrupt cells of her victim tore each other apart.

They were already dead, but that made no difference to her.

Fallen or not, angels do not dream, but if she did, Abaddon has her dream of ripe living bodies to toy with now.

She wouldn't waste her time on simple violence. Wanton bloodshed bored her while pestilence was a puzzle.

"Someone else is here," I say, scanning the room for any signs of life and coming up empty.

"You're right," Lucifer agrees. "This isn't like Abaddon. Someone else decided to follow and play with her scraps. Belial, if I had to wager."

Michael edges open the double doors that lead into a smaller waiting room, and we follow. A faint rustling comes from behind one of the overturned desks. Lucifer is there in an instant, hauling the middle-aged woman out from under her hiding place. A pair of pale blue scrubs marks her as a nurse. Cowering beside her is a younger man dressed in a blood-stained t-shirt and a pair of ripped jeans.

"What did you see?" he demands.

"Lucifer, she's terrified," Michael protests. Lucifer releases the trembling woman and takes a step back, holding up his hands, but he repeats just as forcefully, "What did you see?"

The woman takes an unsteady step, her eyes fixed on the exit sign. Her companion doesn't move. She runs shaky fingers through her tangled hair, tucking a few greying strands behind her ear. "There were so many at first. Their skin was wrong, like it was burned. . . and their teeth." She whips her head around, reassuring herself that a horde of demons isn't still waiting to snatch her in their jaws.

"There were two of them that looked normal," she continues. "A man and a woman. The woman wanted to know where our research lab was."

"What's in the lab?" Michael asks.

The nurse stands up a bit straighter, pushing aside the horrific things she witnessed for the calm familiarity of her job. "It's a teaching hospital. We have specimens of viruses, bacteria, a bit of everything. The man with her just kept breaking things. . . and people." The no-nonsense exterior fades as her face crumples. "If they didn't give the answer she liked he'd touch them and they just. . . weren't there anymore." Her voice breaks as just what the pink mist blanketing the room used to be finally strikes her. "Oh God," she moans.

"God isn't listening." Lucifer takes a step back, clearing the path to the exit. "Run through that door out into the parking lot. Don't stop. Don't look back. Just go."

The shell-shocked man staggers to his feet, looping his arm around the nurse's waist and dragging her toward the door.

"The lab's on the third floor," he calls as they disappear through the double doors.

"At least we aren't in Atlanta," Lucifer mutters. "It's too much to hope for that they don't have anything nasty here but I don't want to think about what she'd do in the CDC."

We make our way to the stairwell, climbing the two flights of stairs in silence, dreading what we'll find at the top. The stairwell is far too open to hide any more survivors, but Grace still searches around every corner, her hopefulness waning with each passing minute.

A hospital in the center of a large city should be teeming with people, and we've found two.

Two.

Metaphors and memories were all she knew of Hell until now. Spells and dead demons. Possessions and vicious angels. But it was all for a reason. Uriel was an insane zealot, but he had an endgame. For all Brielle's cruelties, she still had a goal.

But this amount death and destruction for its own sake? Each one of them fell out of scorn for the humans and disgust for their weaknesses, and now they're worse than the most vile sinner they tormented in the Pit.

Hell makes demons of us all.

The heavy metal door ahead is labeled with a large 3 in stark white paint. Lucifer eases it open, and the smell hits us first. The antiseptic hospital scent is drowned out by the twin scents of blood and fear. The sound of muffled crying comes from the middle of the room. Half a dozen humans stand huddled together like cattle, each trying to hide behind the other.

Circling around them like a shark testing the waters is Belial.

He looks young, far younger than even Grace, dressed like a truant high school student in ripped jeans and an oversized sweatshirt. Sandy brown hair and a wide smile below bright blue eyes does little to dissuade the image of a fresh faced teenager he portrays.

I suppose Ted Bundy had a pleasing face as well.

In Heaven, Belial was just another Seraphim, just another voice in the choir. He wanted to be noticed, to carve a name for himself in blood if necessary.

He catches sight of Lucifer and that schoolboy grin grows even wider, baring straight white teeth. "Lucifer!" he crows, slapping his hand down onto the nearby reception desk. The humans yelp in fear, backing further away from him as his hand leaves a bloody smear across the white lacquered surface of the nurse's station. "Did you finally come to join the party?"

His grin falters when Michael appears in the doorway, his jaw twitching as he glares at the archangel. "So it's true then," he sneers, all joviality gone. "Azazel said so but I wouldn't believe it until I saw it with my own eyes." He shakes his head in disgust. "You're on Heaven's side."

"I'm on my side," Lucifer counters. From one step to the next, Lucifer's entire demeanor shifts. All the light is siphoned out of the room leaving a vacuum as cold and barren as the space between the stars.

This is an archangel. This is *the* archangel.

He let himself feel, let himself love and live as they do, and we let ourselves forget just what Lucifer is. I think even he let himself forget for a time.

Belial's mocking smile doesn't change, but I know he feels it too. The pressure around us all grows, thickening the air, squeezing our lungs, and it's a reminder.

He was the first. And he will bow to no one.

Michael blocks the doorway, and before Belial can notice me he reaches backward and shoves me to the left. I knock into Grace, pushing both of us out of sight of the door.

Michael follows Lucifer into the fray, leaving the door cracked open behind him.

For all that I might resent being relegated to hiding in a stairwell, Michael didn't become Heaven's most feared warrior by lacking in strategy. Underestimating those Fallen got us into this situation in the first place.

I swallow my pride and press my eye against the opening. Grace's heartbeat pounds against my back as she cranes her neck to try and see what's happening without alerting Belial to our presence.

It's an unneeded precaution. Belial doesn't spare a glance back at the door once Michael enters the room. One bloodied hand darts out, snatching the person closest to him by the back of his neck, a tall man in navy scrubs. In a surprising show of bravery, the doctor tries to wriggle away, muttering a litany of broken prayers in Spanish. Belial indulges his attempts for a minute, giggling like a fool as the human fights for his life before finally backhanding him. The prayers fade into quiet whimpers.

"What do you think, Lucifer?" Belial purrs. "Should I make this one go *pop* like all the others or go a bit slower this time? Maybe rip his organs out bit by bit and see how many he can identify? There's sin in this one. He's fair game." Belial yanks the taller man's head down lower. "Greed *and* envy! So much cheating all stemming from those two little sins. Cheats on his taxes, cheats on his husband, even cheating on his medical boards. That one haunts him. I was never as good at reading the cattle as you are, Lucifer, but I think that's the gist of it."

"Enough!"

Belial's laughter cuts off abruptly as Lucifer takes a step closer to him. Belial flinches, the childish swagger draining from him the closer Lucifer gets. "You forget yourself," he spits. "You forget who owns you."

Belial tries to muster up another laugh at this, but it sounds hollow and tinged with more than a bit of fear. "You?"

"Hell."

Belial falters, his grip loosening on the man and Lucifer takes full advantage to stalk closer until Belial is barely an arm's length away. "Poor little Belial," Lucifer mocks. "No mind of your own, no creativity. I'm not surprised to see you here playing with the crumbs Abaddon leaves behind. *The Fallen Angel of Chaos*. Did you give yourself that title? I certainly didn't. I never wanted you in Hell's court at all, but Azazel did want an errand boy, and you were always so eager to please anyone with power."

"You think you can get inside of my head? It won't work."

"It already has."

Belial smiles again, but the cocksure attitude is gone from his face, leaving nothing but a child hiding behind bravado. "Do you really think you can stop us? Abaddon's down the hall cooking up something fun." He squeezes his captive's neck just a bit tighter. The man's eyes bulge outward as his tormented lungs scream for oxygen. "I was supposed to round up everyone left for her test subjects, but I got bored." Belial shrugs. "How many can she really need?"

Lucifer's voice is deadly cold. "You have a choice, Belial. You can go back to Hell or you can die. I won't make the offer again." Belial hesitates, and I know Lucifer has him.

For all that he revels in death and destruction, Belial has always been a follower. He enjoyed it in Hell, as much as it could be enjoyed because there he could imagine himself royalty, forcing the demons to call him *Lord Belial* without a hint of irony. With Lucifer gone, Belial would have rejoiced in the chance to vie for his mantle.

Sad little king of a sad little hill.

But the rest of them wanted out, and Azazel would never

leave her well-trained pet behind when he might be useful topside.

Even if all she planned to use him for was cannon fodder.

"What is Azazel plotting?" Lucifer demands.

"Nothing." Belial's reply is far too quick to be believed.

Lucifer is on him before he can blink, wrenching his hostage away and slamming Belial's face into the floor hard enough to crack the tiles.

Behind me, Grace gasps. This is a side she's only seen of Lucifer in the long buried memories Elissa's spell dug up. This isn't the Lightbringer who lit the stars and claimed the title of God's favorite. This isn't Lucifer who laid down his life for love of a human.

This is the Devil, and he will make us all remember that.

Belial struggles to rise, his face a bloody mess, but Lucifer presses his heel in the center of his back, pinning Belial to the floor like a trapped bug. "Stay down. You belong on your knees." When Belial doesn't attempt to buck him off, he circles around the prone angel and crouches by his head before speaking, his voice a low rasp. "I should just kill you now and release you from your pathetic existence, but I don't know if I feel like mercy today."

Lucifer unsheathes his blade, the bright metal gleaming. He runs the tip down Belial's back achingly slow. "Maybe I'll cut off your wings and leave you here with the humans." Lucifer drags the tip of the blade back upward, pressing against his shoulder blade and my own wings ache at the image. "This blade is one of Michael's. Forged in Heaven. Tell me Belial, what do you think would happen if I took your wings at the root with this? Would it turn you into one of them? Weak and mortal, bound to the Earth?"

"She wants to take Heaven!"

Lucifer's hand freezes, the blade pressing deeper into

Belial's shoulder. "Of course she does," he mutters before raising his voice. "Where is she?"

When Belial doesn't immediately answer Lucifer drags him upright, twisting his bloodied visage to face him. "WHERE?" he repeats.

"Gone," Belial stammers through his split lips. "The witch told her everything she needed to do. Azazel said she was leaving this city to us."

I go cold. "What witch?" I whisper to no one, even though I know the answer.

"What witch?" Michael unknowingly echoes my words.

Belial doesn't even look at Michael. All of his focus, all of his fear is on Lucifer. "The dead one," he answers. "The one that opened the door."

Lucifer releases his grip on Belial, shoving him away like he's touching something disgusting. Without prompting, Belial drops to his knees on the floor, his head bowed in supplication.

Lucifer looks over at our hiding spot, but I know he's not looking at me. He's searching for a pair of wide grey eyes.

Whatever he sees, he doesn't hesitate anymore. He jams the blade through the back of Belial's neck, severing his spine and killing him before his body even strikes the floor.

The blade slips out of Lucifer's hand and clatters onto the tiles. The jarring noise brings the terrified humans back to their senses enough that they sprint from the room, nearly knocking each other down in their haste to reach the stairwell. They slam open the door, pushing past us both as if we were invisible, and clatter down the stairs, abject terror making any effort at silence impossible.

With Belial dead, there's no more reason for Grace and me to stay out of sight, but after I take a few steps into the room I freeze.

Belial's corpse lays on the floor between us, and my feet won't let me take another step closer.

"You were always so eager to please anyone with power."

"Stay down. You belong on your knees."

Too close to the words the false Lucifer taunted me with in Hell. Far too close.

Grace stops short beside me, and it takes me a minute to register what Lucifer's muttering to himself. "I should have known. Where else would that witch end up? Of course, Azazel would find her interesting." He grabs the blade from the ground and turns to us.

"Belial wanted to go back to Hell. He's back there now."

"How?" Grace asks. I steal a glance at her, and her face is shuttered, blank. She chose the Devil, and I think she's only just now understanding what that means.

Hope is written across Lucifer's face but he doesn't take a step closer. He doesn't try to touch her, and when he speaks it sounds like every word pains him. "We have souls too, Grace." Then he takes a breath, and he's all business again. "Belial gets the chance to enjoy Hell from the other side now. Maybe he'll end up in a cell next to Uriel."

Lucifer casts one last unreadable look at Grace before walking toward the double doors ahead adding, "Belial was always nothing but a lackey. The rest of them won't be this easy."

16

CAILA

Dark.

Cold.

Not again. The panic rises in me like a sickness. It doesn't matter that there is no collar around my throat this time and no chains binding me.

I'm just as trapped.

Row upon row of cells stretches in both directions for as far as I can see. I take a tentative step closer to the nearest one, looking back at the blank space where the portal I came through moments ago used to be.

There's really no going back.

I raise my hand to touch the heavy iron bolt holding the door shut, but I shrink back before my fingers brush the metal.

Then I see it, that tear in the fabric between the worlds. The red glow seems to come from miles down the endless corridor like a distant forest fire. I start moving toward it, following the familiar tug of the magic, passing door after identical door, each one leading into someone's private torment. It's dizzying in its sameness but I forget all about doors and cells when I finally reach it.

This rift is so much larger than the tiny portal Elissa created or even the one we found in the alley. It stretches end to end across the corridor, pulsing and throbbing like a heartbeat as it grows.

I press my hand against it. It feels alive. It feels like flesh, and it bulges outward into the world. The seal Elissa closed it with is barely holding on. Soon enough, it will break and all of Hell will pour into Earth to drown us all.

Not anymore.

I lean closer, staring through the milky membrane, and I see the alley where the swell of demons over-ran us. Even then, we were already too late. The Fallen had already made their exits. I blink and my view changes to the docks, then a barren field. One by one, it cycles through every exit point.

Six. She made six.

We never would have found them all in time, and even if we had it wouldn't have been enough.

"His blood opened it. Yours will close it."

Elissa's knife is still clutched in my hand, her dried blood tacky on the blade.

She was right. I know what I have to do.

I hardly feel the slice down my forearm, but I know that the scent of fresh, living blood will draw the demons to me like sharks smelling a fresh kill. I press my hand against the flow, not to staunch it but to make certain it's enough.

It's always blood, after all.

Once my fingers are stained deep red I press both palms against the rift. It shudders and writhes beneath my fingers, almost bucking me off as some sentient part of the spell recognizes that I'm the being that can end it.

You'll be trapped here.

Just step through the door.

Say you failed.
No one will be surprised.
You're weak.

I grit my teeth and push harder against it, drowning out the whispers in my head as Brielle's spell tries to slither inside.

Nothing seems to happen for too long. When it begins, it's such a subtle change that I nearly miss it. The ragged edges of the rift knit back together like a wound and the bright red light that glowed in the darkness like infection grows paler.

I don't look away. I don't even blink. My focus is so intent on watching the tiny increments of progress as the rift heals that I nearly fall forward when it vanishes into nothing.

I did it.

The gates are closed.

I look around and see nothing but door after door in both directions, none of them leading anywhere I want to visit.

What do I do now?

I WALK.

While the routes through Eden twist and turn, the trails as meandering as a river, the constant monotony of the corridor is already beginning to eat at my mind. I know Hell is far more than just this single hallway, but how do I reach it?

I skid to a stop in front of one of the doors, scrutinizing it for the tiniest indication that it might lead anywhere else. Scattered at seemingly random intervals among the doors are a few with a single difference.

No bolts.

Steeling myself, I push open the door, clutching Elissa's blade tightly enough to turn my bloodstained knuckles white.

I step across the threshold and find myself in Eden.

"How?" I murmur as the door slams behind me.

But while my mind says *Eden*, I know better. What surrounds me is a pale mockery of the beauty of the Garden.

No matter which way I turn, my surroundings look like the aftermath of a forest fire. Every color has been swallowed up by black and grey. Barren trees reach their charred limbs toward a sky the color of ashes. Even the air smells of smoke and decay.

I follow the path as it twines its way through the blackened trees, and I see the bones of beauty beneath the ugliness and death of this place. This place sprung from the memory of the Garden, warped by darkness and pain. It should be frightening, the sinister forest of a child's nightmare, but there's such a sadness that wraps around every patch of scorched grass and dying tree.

I know this is Lucifer's work. In every step, I feel the Morningstar's presence as surely as if he walked beside me. This is his memory of Heaven or as much of it as he could create within Hell.

For the first moment since Elissa showed me that book and sealed my fate, I'm not afraid.

I pass a small clearing, the tall grass grey and brittle. Dotted among the barren stems are tiny white flowers, bright as snow against the landscape.

"Asphodel," I whisper. The only flower that grows in the underworld. On Earth, it's rare beyond the telling of it, the stuff of legends and myths and a crucial ingredient to more than a few spells. I pluck a handful from the ground, tucking them into my pockets to give to Elissa when I return.

If I return.

Just as in the true Eden, this false Eden lulls me into calm far too easily. I force myself to put one foot in front of the other, though the unrelenting grey entices me to lay down and close my eyes. To rest. To forget.

I follow the path, and with each step the ground grows more and more studded with bleached white rocks. The surface is as uneven as cobblestones, and after nearly tripping for a third time I stop to stare at a large stone jutting from the hard-packed soil.

I crouch down and brush away the dust, freezing when I realize that the angular rock isn't a rock at all.

It's a vertebra. I stand up quickly, turning in a circle and staring at the ground around me and seeing femurs, metacarpals, jawbones all laid down like a carpet.

I hear the sound of feet ahead of me, and a figure comes into view over the rise. The thick screen of trees has opened up into even more barren fields, and there's nowhere to hide.

The last thing I expect is to recognize who shuffles past me.

"Uriel?"

He glances at me for a moment, his brow furrowing as a mind made sluggish by death tries to connect the dots of who I am. Whatever memories or images his brain manages to conjure up, they aren't enough to keep his attention focused on me. After a minute he blinks and continues his lumbering walk down the path until he disappears into the trees.

"Don't take it personally. He ignores me too."

My head snaps up at the voice, and I gape at the figure that appeared seemingly out of nowhere. He's standing just off the path, the dried grass brushing against his calves. He smiles as if pleased that some creature in this place is actually acknowledging him, and he steps onto the path.

He's taller than I am, and his long legs make quick work of the distance between us. There's no fear in him. This is not some timid soul, cowed by torment. He walks with the authority of a man accustomed to being obeyed, an aristocrat or at least very skilled pretender.

His clothes speak of another time – a brocade jacket hastily pulled over an untucked white shirt, deep blue trousers that hug a slim waist and soft brown riding boots speckled with ash. Even from a few feet away, I can tell the fineness of the material of each article. When he lived, this was a man who wanted his wealth known.

Russet hair falls in gentle waves around his jawbone, and his slate-blue eyes twinkle with amusement under my scrutiny.

"I'm Roux," he offers.

"Roux," I echo, my voice growing tighter as I realize why he seems familiar and a stranger all at the same time. Brielle's Roux. The one whose death began it all.

Roux comes closer, the uneven ground beneath our feet failing to phase him. His eyes narrow as he takes me in. "You're alive," he murmurs, wonder coloring his voice. "How are you here? Why are you here?" He moves closer until he's well within my space. I should want to back away, to put any amount of distance between myself and the man that monster so adored, but I see nothing resembling a threat in Roux's actions. It's nothing more than genuine curiosity.

I'm something *new*.

"Where is here?"

Roux sighs. "Don't tell me I'm the one that has to have the 'Hell' talk with you?"

I shake my head, and Roux smiles, relief evident in his wide grin. "Good. This is his Hell anyway." He tilts his head down the path where Uriel disappeared. "Apparently he was quite the gardener in his former life. Hell didn't quite know what to do with the soul of an archangel, so they sent him here. I guess this is the VIP suite."

I chuckle but remind myself that however disarming Roux

may be, I need to stay on guard. "You didn't learn that in Napoleonic France."

Roux grins, but I don't miss the flicker of questioning in his eyes at my offhand remark. "I listen."

"Why are you in Uriel's Hell?"

Roux shrugs. He walks back to the edge of the path, staring out at the vast, dead grassland. "I was here first. I like this place." He glances back at me. "I never did anything bad enough to warrant one of those rooms, but I can't very well leave. Heaven sent me here so they certainly won't have me, and it sounds dreadfully boring anyway. I wouldn't go if they begged me." His voice lowers to a hush. "And now she's here."

She. I shudder at the mention of Brielle.

Roux notices. "You know me, don't you? Or her." I nod but say nothing. "I forget things. This place does that to you. It's easy to drift away." He trails off, and I wonder just what ephemeral memories he's trying to call up. "She did terrible things after I died, didn't she? Elissa tried to warn me, but I didn't want to believe it of her. We were happy, the two of us and then the three of us. The world was ours." Roux's attention drifts back to the barren fields. "I like it here. It reminds me of the fields in winter just before the snows came."

He looks back at me. "The Devil made this place. He came here quite a bit before the other one showed up. I think he liked the quiet, but I never asked. I can tell when a man needs solitude."

"Where does this path go?" Roux blinks, before turning back to the field as though he's forgotten I was here.

He steps off the path, and the dry cracking of the stems beneath his feet sounds impossibly loud in the silence.

"To the end," he replies without looking at me. "Or it might be the beginning." This time when he walks away, I don't stop him.

I continue down the path, and soon the open fields give

way to denser vegetation. Snarls of brambles and thorn bushes blanket the ground like something from a fairy tale.

Some tiny ember within me says that I'm going the right way. I hope it's Elissa's magic or angelic intuition, but I'm more than a little bit terrified that it's nothing more than wishful thinking.

The path grows smaller and smaller with each step as the tangled brush encroaches on the bare soil. The thorns catch at my clothes and tear my skin as I pass.

Go back, this place seems to say.

Turn away.

Leave.

But I don't allow myself to pause.

No angel has been to the end of Eden, but I will find the end of Hell's Garden.

The brambles grow even thicker, the space between the rows even tighter and I spread my wings, trying to beat back the clawing branches.

It's so dark. The branches rise up like dead fingers on either side of me, blotting out even the dim grey light of the washed out sky. Above me, they reach out to each other, the thorn-tipped ends almost touching.

What I'm treading on can barely be called a path, but I put one foot in front of the other, fighting my rising dread when a few steps later the branches finally make contact above my head.

I'm alone. I can see less and less of what's around me. The canopy of blackened wood above me lets in only the faintest illumination from the wan light outside, and my brain screams for me to turn back while I still can.

What if I'm trapped here, pinned in the branches like a lost bird?

I almost wish for demons, for the Fallen, for Brielle's torments. Anything but this immobilization.

I twist my body against the grasping plants, fighting to take just another step forward until I feel something give way.

I pitch forward into nothingness, ending up sprawled gracelessly on the ground. The rough rock tears into my already mangled hands, but I hardly notice the added pain as I stare around at the clearing I've fallen into.

Behind me is the lattice of thorns hemming me in against the sheer rock face. Already the broken limbs that marked my passage are righting themselves, slipping back into an impenetrable wall. In front of me is a sheer cliff face. There are no openings, no hidden doors. Nothing but raw black stone.

Trapped.

I swallow, feeling the panic rise in me like bile until I tilt my head back and see the stars.

The tiny circle of brightness is miles above, and I crane my neck to stare at the pinpricks of light so far away.

I push myself slowly to my feet, feeling every scratch and cut and embedded thorn. Hell is for suffering, after all. If you heal too quickly the pain stops.

My wings already ache at the thought of the sheer flight upward to free myself, and I lean against the stone and let the weariness overtake me, at least for the moment.

The clearing is dark, the shadows deep, but it's not the unrelenting blackness of my cell, and it takes me a moment to register just where the faint illumination is coming from.

A mess of bloody feathers is scattered like tainted snow across the stone, the red streaks stark against the pristine white plumes. Half the feathers are charred to the point of looking unrecognizable.

This is where he fell.

I look upward again at that immeasurable distance and I can almost see Lucifer falling, his wings mangled into uselessness by the brother he loved. The pain when he landed must have been immeasurable. Even for an immortal, that kind of brutal agony leaves scars.

I think of him laying here, every bone pulverized into dust, and feeling every agonizing moment as shattered bones and ruptured tissues knit themselves back together.

Our wings always take the longest time to heal. Even after every other piece of him had repaired itself, Lucifer still spent his first days in Hell dragging his destroyed wings behind him.

I wonder if he thought they'd stay broken forever.

Phenex followed this same path, stepping out into the empty air and letting himself fall into perdition behind Lucifer.

I think of them both leaving this place behind and then Lucifer burying it in thorns and briars, hiding it from the rest of Hell like some secret he wants to forget.

I crouch down and pick up one of the feathers. It glows, the stark white so much brighter than even Michael's wings. The Heavenly luminescence lights up the darkness as bright as the stars. After all, he did create them. Even blood and ash can't dim the Lightbringer.

I stretch my wings, wincing as the movement tugs on my damaged muscles. It's a long flight upward to reach Heaven's borders, but there's no other choice. This way back is lost to them both – the Morningstar and the Phoenix.

But not me. Not yet.

I fly upward, clenching one of Lucifer's lost feathers in my hand. My eyes are barely more than slits as the air rushes over them, but I welcome the sting that washes the dank, dead air of Hell from my lungs. My wings throb with each beat that takes me higher. The air around me grows thin and cool, and my strength is ebbing, blood loss and exhaustion and fear all taking a toll on even my angelic resilience.

Then I think of Lucifer alone in this place with his shattered wings. I think of Elissa alone in those first days with her shattered heart. I think of Phenex alone in that cell.

Heaven and Hell broke us all, but we survived. We thrived. We *healed*.

Even as my wings falter and I lose a few precious feet, I dig down until I find the last scrap of energy in me. The stars are so close now. At least this part of this nightmare is almost at an end.

I burst through the mouth of the tunnel and out into the night, collapsing onto the stones at the edge of the Pit. The stars blink down at me, so much closer than on Earth. I lay on the bare stones where the archangels fought, my lungs still heaving. All around me, the stones still bear the marks of that terrible fight.

Some scars will never heal.

But they do fade.

I stagger to my feet and stare down into that maw of darkness.

I did it. I really did it.

I know I should rest and give my body the chance to heal before even attempting to leave, but I want nothing so badly as to be *home*.

Home with the sudden strange role reversal of Elissa acting like a mother hen and the heat in Phenex's eyes when he looks at me. Ignoring my body's call for respite just a little longer, I point my wings toward Iberville Street.

I've rested long enough.

17

PHENEX

No one speaks.

Lucifer stalks through the double doors up ahead without looking back. Belial's corpse lays crumpled like a broken doll under the flickering fluorescent lights. Grace looks shaken as she follows without a word, leaving Michael and me to bring up the rear.

A hospital this size should be choked with people. Half a dozen hallways branch off from the central corridor in each direction like arteries. They should be filled with doctors and nurses, patients and their families. It should be loud, dozens of voices making themselves heard over the metallic beeps of heart monitors and other machines.

It's silent as a tomb and just as lacking in warm bodies. We pass abandoned beds, their occupant's IV bags still dripping on the floor. We step around broken bodies, trying not to think too hard of what happened to these poor souls in a place of healing.

We even find a few survivors, terrified clusters of patients or staff hiding in supply closets or wedged inside the tiny patient bathrooms. Michael ushers them out of their hiding spots and toward the stairwell, and they obey his commands without asking who he is or what happened to their safe little world, the shell-shocked looks in their eyes already showing the scars this day has left.

Grace scarcely notices them. She scans the face of each survivor quickly before moving on, and she makes sure to inspect every dead body she passes as she searches for her missing friend. She buries her usual compassion under a wall of detachment that won't hold for long.

The lab is tucked away in the farthest corner of the third floor like an unwanted secret, and our progress is slow. Grace pauses to peer into every empty room we pass with a grim look never leaving her face. Abruptly she veers down one corridor, shoving open the swinging doors that read "OR – Staff Only."

Lucifer sighs, changing his course to follow her. The Devil walks a few steps behind Grace as if he's afraid to get too close after what she just witnessed, and it sets my nerves on edge even more. The last thing we need is to splinter apart after everything we've already endured.

And everything still in front of us.

Grace cautiously peers into one operating room after another. The first two are blessedly empty, but when she cracks the third door she lets out a sharp gasp of "Andre!" and shoves it open.

The room is a mess. Surgical tools are flung across the floor, the bright metal of the scalpels glinting under the harsh lights. A tangle of electronic debris from the smashed monitors fills one corner of the room; two dead women in navy blue scrubs are slumped in the other.

And strapped to the operating table, his arms spread wide like some twisted modern crucifixion is Andre.

Grace is by his side in an instant, yanking on the restraints, her fingers fumbling with the buckles. Her movement rouses Andre from whatever stupor he's in and he wakes up with a loud wheeze, the air rattling unhealthily in his lungs as he struggles to get away from her.

"Andre. Andre! It's Grace. It's me. You're safe." Grace runs her hand over his sweaty forehead, trying to get him to look at her.

His eyes are wide and wild, the whites bloodshot and red, and he can't seem to fully focus on anything. His gaze bounces from the door to me to Lucifer before he's finally able to settle on Grace.

"No one's safe," he whispers, his voice hoarse.

I go cold when I realize that the sheen of sweat coating his skin isn't just a byproduct of stress or the airless room, and the glazed look in his eyes isn't just from trauma. I see no injuries, no blood decorating his pale blue scrubs. Grace unfastens the final buckle holding him down, but he doesn't try to move or sit up.

He's infected with something and knowing Abaddon, it's nothing humanity has a handy vaccine for.

"What did she give you?" I ask.

Andre looks over at me, the fog around his mind seeming to clear for an instant before deepening even more. "Don't know. Everything was chaos. There were monsters. That's what they were, weren't they? Monsters." Andre rambles, his thick tongue stumbling over his speech.

"And everyone ran. I hid in the lab, and when she came to the door, I thought she was a patient looking for somewhere to hide. I let her in." Andre flinches as if speaking of Abaddon will conjure her back into the room. "I asked her if she had seen what was happening, and she just kept smiling. She looked around, and all I could think of was a kid in a candy store. Then I couldn't talk anymore. I couldn't move."

He scrunches his eyes shut and it's like watching a child trying to will themselves into invisibility. If only closing his eyes would undo whatever she did to him. "She kept saying humans always talk about how terrible disease is when we're the worst plague of all." Andre lifts his arm, his movements sluggish as if the limb was made of lead. He scrubs a trembling hand across his face before dropping it down to hang limply at his side.

"She tried to open the sample fridge, and the alarm went off. You need a keycard. But she just ripped the door off like it was nothing," his voice grows more slurred with each word as he fights to stay conscious.

"What do they have here?" Lucifer interrupts.

"Not a lot, but enough," Andre mumbles. "No ebola, but I know we have malaria, TB, a few nastier strains of influenza." Andre's voice breaks off in a coughing fit. He can't catch his breath, and his eyes bulge as his lungs fight to take in any oxygen at all. We watch helplessly until the hacking coughs finally die down to a weak wheeze. A few drops of blood are flecked across his lips.

Lucifer leans closer. "Andre, do you know where she is?"

Andre's voice sounds like he gargled with broken glass when he speaks. Every word has to be brutally painful on his ravaged throat, but he's still aware enough to realize the importance of what we're asking. "She said the Devil was coming to stop her. She said she felt it when you closed the door and that she wanted another one. A better one."

"Elissa," There's no masking the alarm in Michael's voice, and even I can tell he's seconds away from spreading his wings and tearing his way back to Iberville Street.

It's the low rumble of Lucifer's voice that reels in that rising panic. "Grace, you know you can heal him. You've healed much, much worse." He turns to Michael. "You know you can do the same for what ails him. This isn't some natural human malady. We all know that. Whatever Abaddon injected into him, she corrupted it with her *special gifts* first."

He plucks the discarded syringe from the floor, a viscous black fluid coating the barrel. "Look for the darkness, and draw it out of him. Both of you."

Michael casts one more nervous look at the door, his mind already with Elissa, but he keeps his protests silent.

Elissa's wards are strong. They won't keep Abaddon out forever, but they'll be enough to hold her at bay until we get there.

She has time. Andre doesn't.

"I don't know if I can do this." The quaver in Grace's voice feels wrong. She healed Lucifer. She healed me, dragging us both back from the very brink of death. She never shied away from walking into Brielle's house of horrors or her part in the spell that nearly snapped her mind.

"You can." Lucifer is at her side, the distance between them forgotten as he twists one blonde curl around his fingertip. "You can do this," he breathes. He looks up long enough to meet Michael's eyes and nods.

Out of the archangels, Raphael was always the healer. Michael caused wounds, he didn't fix them, but any good soldier knows his fair share of battlefield medicine.

Only those that have not Fallen can heal.

Whoever this human is, he doesn't deserve this. He doesn't deserve to die an excruciating death as a pawn in a celestial pissing match.

So many dead already, and I can't even fathom how many more will follow.

So we'll start by saving just this one.

Grace presses one hand flat against Andre's cheek before running her fingertip over his neck, searching for the tiny puncture mark where Abaddon forced the toxin into him.

Such a small thing to cause so much damage.

Michael follows her lead, resting his palm on Andre's clammy forehead. His other hand presses down on his shoulder immobilizing him on the table as surely as if he were still strapped down.

Deep furrows form in Grace's brow as she stares down in concentration.

"Am I going to die?" Andre whimpers.

Grace's eyes widen. "No," she answers quickly. There's no hesitance in her voice this time. "I see it."

"Draw it to you." Lucifer is just over her shoulder, his voice a silken whisper in her ear. "Darkness always follows the light."

Andre's veins pulse on every patch of visible skin, inky threads of Abaddon's mutated virus slithering through them like living creatures.

Then I notice the light.

It's faint, and I almost question my eyes. But I remember it, that golden radiance that suffused me when she brought me back, warm fire brightening my tattered soul. I followed that light back from the edge of death, and I would have flown into the sun and burned my wings to cinders like Icarus to reach it.

For all her evil, a tiny part of Abaddon is still an angel, and the virus in Andre's veins is a part of her.

And darkness always follows the light.

Grace draws it closer to her, tempting the virus to abandon Andre's ravaged cells and slide upward through his veins like a billion silent predators. Her presence and the lure of attacking an archangel are more than enough enticement.

The first drop seeps out of the puncture. More and more blackened teardrops of the infernal poison flow down his neck as Grace pulls the virus from his veins. Andre writhes on the table, pain and fear warring with his muddled brain, and his body begins to convulse as the virus tries to fight through its death throes.

"Don't stop," Michael growls through gritted teeth,

pushing Andre back against the unyielding surface of the operating table.

Grace doesn't. Her eyes narrow to slits as she stares unblinkingly at Andre, scanning every square inch of his form for a single rogue virus trying to elude her.

Abruptly Andre stills, slumping back onto the cold metal table as the fight drains out of him.

"What did I do?" Grace asks, alarm raising her voice. "Did I kill him?"

Michael shakes his head, lifting his hands off Andre's body long enough to check his pulse. "He just passed out. You did it, Grace."

Grace smiles weakly. None of us will know what permanent damages Abaddon's little experiment might have wrought on her friend until he wakes up.

We don't have the luxury of patting ourselves on the back just yet.

Now that Andre is out of the woods, Michael is already halfway out the door. "We need to get back to Elissa," he begins.

Lucifer cuts him off before he can get out another word. "*I* need you to get both of them back to Grace's house." Lucifer continues on over Michael's protests as if he doesn't hear them. "Phenex and I can handle Abaddon, especially if Elissa's there as well. But if something goes wrong, you are our backup. *Both* of you. And there's still Caila. If she did close the gate, that's one less worry, but Hell is a maze. It's meant to be impossible to escape, even if you aren't supposed to be there. Worst case scenario, someone needs to be alive to get her out."

Lucifer grasps Michael's arm. "I won't let her be harmed, brother, and you know as well as I do that Elissa can more than handle herself."

Nodding stiffly, Michael scoops up Andre's limp form and leaves with Grace on his heels.

Lucifer turns to me, the fires of Hell burning in his eyes. "Let's end this."

TAP. Tap. Tap.

The security gate rattles as Abaddon raps on the metal. She looks out of place in the neighborhood, like a census taker or a social worker lost on the wrong street. An unadorned navy suit hugs her slim body, the conservative skirt ending just past her knees. Deep auburn hair the color of old blood pulled back in a tight bun rounds off the severe look.

Only her right hand marks her as something *other*. Her index finger is wrapped in Hell-forged metal, intricate armor that resembles blackened scales ending in a razor sharp tip. It's that metallic nail tapping on Elissa's front door.

Lucifer and I watch, perched on the roof of the house next door, crouched beside lost Frisbees and dead leaves.

"I know you're in there, witch, and I know what you did," she calls, a sing-song lilt in her voice. "I can smell the stink of the Hell-bound from a mile away, and you reek of it." She curls her fingers through the warped metal of the gate and shakes the door on its hinges.

"Go in through the back, and check on Elissa," Lucifer hisses. "Wait for my signal."

I circle around to the rear of the house, thankful for once of the abundance of burned-out streetlights. I ease open the back door as silently as the old hinges will allow, feeling the whisper of magic that rushes over me as I enter. The wards are still holding.

Sprawled on her back, the carefully placed salt scattered across the floor, is Elissa.

"Elissa?" When she doesn't move, I rush to her, hauling her limp body onto my lap and shaking her. Too many seconds tick by before she blinks her pale blue eyes blearily at me. She's herself again.

"Phenex? How–" Her voice breaks off when she notices the circle broken around us, and her face falls. "I had her," she whispers. "I felt her close the rift. . . she closed them all. I had her, but the connection was so weak once it closed. I was trying to guide her back to me, but then it just snapped, and everything went dark."

My heart sinks. Caila, my Caila, lost in Hell.

The gate rattles again, louder this time, and the whole house shudders as the wards start to buckle under her pressure.

"Who?" Elissa mouths, pulling herself to her feet.

"Abaddon. She's not exactly happy that you closed the gate. Azazel and Brielle had a little meet and greet in Hell, so she knows how to make another. She just needs a witch."

If Elissa's afraid, she doesn't show it. Her jaw tightens, and I'm amazed the glare she casts toward the door doesn't melt the metal under Abaddon's hands. She checks the small of her back for her daggers and sighs when she only pulls one from the hidden holster.

Caila has the other.

"Backup?"

"Lucifer. Abaddon got to Grace's friend first, but he'll live. Michael and Grace are with him."

Elissa rolls her shoulders and tightens her grip on the dagger. "You, me, and Lucifer? I'm okay with those odds." Before I can react, Elissa strides to the door. A flick of her wrist and I feel the wards drop. "Let her come."

She wrenches open the door and catches Abaddon in the

chest with one booted foot. The Fallen angel staggers back a few feet but recovers quickly.

Lucifer lands behind her. "Wait for my signal?" he asks with bland amusement.

Despite the situation, Elissa can't resist a wry quip. "When have I ever taken direction well?"

At Lucifer's voice, Abaddon whirls to face him. "Lucifer!" She's all smiles as she descends the steps, her no-nonsense grey heels silent on the cement. She leaves her back vulnerable to Elissa and me in a way that says she doesn't consider either of us a legitimate threat.

Lucifer regards her coldly. "It's over for you, Abaddon. Belial's dead, so there will be no one rushing to your aid tonight. And you are no Azazel."

"Did he die?" Abaddon asks, the saccharine tone of her voice unconcerned with Lucifer's threats. "That handsome nurse. I didn't have much to work with, but a good chef uses whatever ingredients are on hand to create a masterpiece." Her head snaps around to catch Elissa creeping closer. "Try it, witch, and every human in this street will start their day tomorrow by coughing up blood."

"You're bluffing," I say, "You're not Pestilence. You can't create a plague from nothing."

"Can't I?" she mocks. "Care to test it? There must be at least a hundred or so test subjects on this street. Poor, innocent humans sleeping in their beds. No idea what's waiting outside."

No one moves.

"Then we seem to be at a stalemate." She turns back to Lucifer. "Such a pity. It would have been fun making this world bleed with you again. It would have been like old times." The fake sweetness drops away as her face twists into something ugly. "Father chose them over us, but I never expected the same of you."

Lucifer doesn't react. "How does it feel knowing Azazel left you behind for the wolves?"

"You think you can get inside my head, Lucifer? I'm not some fragile little soul begging for forgiveness to make the pain stop." She turns to me, her lips curling up into a cruel smile. Over her shoulder, I see Michael land beside Lucifer, but the presence of a second archangel does little to comfort me as Abaddon takes another step closer.

"And you. The Devil's right hand weeping in a cell. You know, he called for you, Lucifer. I think he forgot his own name before he stopped screaming yours. But he never came for you, did he Phenex? You and that pretty little morsel the witch brought in. Asmodeus wanted a turn at her, but it was so much more fun to just watch you two fumble in the darkness."

They watched. They laughed at us.

I wait for the familiar feeling, the blood pounding in my ears, the tightness in my chest, the phantom feeling of the collar around my neck. I wait for the disgust at myself for my own reactions.

It's there. Some part of it will always be there, scars etched into my soul as surely as the scar was carved into my throat. But I can't afford to crumble now, not when Abaddon's staring down at me, and Caila's lost inside Hell.

"I'll give you the same choice I gave Belial. Return to Hell or die."

"Neither." Abaddon strikes before I can think, darting like a snake and sealing her lips against mine. It's nothing more than her breath that passes between us, but I can't help thinking of mustard gas or Sarin, chemical warfare choking the city as it slumbers.

She pulls away, dodging the stab from Elissa's blade that would have disemboweled her. She dances back a few feet, close enough for Michael and Lucifer to strike, but neither of them are looking at her.

I try to take a breath, and my lungs won't move. I can already feel the paralysis creeping downward, faster with each pound of my already struggling heart. My legs give out underneath me as the muscles seize up and I topple to the ground.

"This won't kill me," I gasp, wasting that last precious bit of air on her.

"No," Abaddon agrees, smirking down at me. "It won't. Your whole body will shut down, but your mind will still be alive in there. Just like back home, locked away in the darkness."

I can feel my throat closing up and my chest tightening, and I can't tell anymore if the dizziness is from whatever Abaddon did or the panic attack cresting over me. I'm denied even the luxury of shaking. I lay still, staring up at the muted light of the stars, locked inside my own body.

Not this. Not again. Anything but this.

Kill me instead.

When I broke in Hell, there was nothing. I slipped away into the hidden corners of my mind, and I was gone. There was no awareness, no silent mental screams.

When I broke, I wasn't a prisoner anymore. I wasn't *Phenex* anymore. I was nothing. I was no one.

This is so much worse.

Every sound is muffled, as though even my eardrums are paralyzed, but I hear the scuffling of feet on broken asphalt and the clash of metal on metal. Three against one should be an easy fight, but none of them know what other tricks she might be hiding.

A voice that isn't Lucifer or Michael bellows, "Abaddon!" and I hear the sick thud of a fist striking flesh with enough force to shatter bone.

I can't move, can't blink, can't even draw a breath to

scream. The burn in my lungs is unrelenting as every cell screams in agony for oxygen that won't come.

A shadow passes over me, and my tearing eyes struggle to focus on the blurry figure in front of me. Maybe it's death that's finally come for me. There's no Grace to pull me from the edge this time.

"Shhhh," the figure whispers. Soft fingers card through my hair, and I think that Abaddon must be more powerful than I realized. I must really be dying because the voice sounds like *hers*, and I'm sure she's dead. I let her walk into Hell, so I as good as killed her myself.

I stare at the fuzzy shape through my tears. Pale hair and borrowed black clothes, all shot through with red. Her skin and clothes and even her wings are tattered and bloody but she's alive.

Whole.

As suddenly as the torment began, whatever hold Abaddon has on me snaps. The sound roars back into my dampened ears, and I hear Lucifer's voice screaming, "Let him go or I'll take the other one!" I gasp as I jerk upright, sucking air violently into my frozen lungs. I start coughing, and I can't stop as my body restarts itself. The cramped muscles of my chest shake with every wheezing cough until I nearly retch, but I can move. I'm alive.

I blink rapidly until my eyes clear enough to make out Caila's face, her cheeks streaked with blood and ash and tears like she just crawled through Hell because *she did*.

I want to kiss her and drag her into my arms and never let her go again.

But first, this.

I stagger to my feet, leaning on Caila's shoulder heavily, and take in the scene around me. Abaddon is on her knees, that pristine suit looking more than a little worse for wear.

Her wings are out, or they were. One blackened wing is still attached to her shoulder blade

Just one.

The other lies in the street, a bloody mess of feathers still twitching as the severed nerves fire all at once. Abaddon's face is contorted in agony, and for the barest instant, I almost pity her.

For an angel to lose their wings. . . there aren't words to describe that. Even when Michael fought Lucifer and won, Michael broke his wings but he didn't take them. The pain of a lost wing never lessens. It never heals.

If Abaddon were anyone else, she would deserve pity.

Blades from Heaven and Hell never grow dull. They keep their razor edge for eternity. They can cleave muscle or bone like paper. The ragged stump bleeding down Abaddon's back should be as precise as clean as a scalpel cut.

It's not. He made it hurt.

Blood coats Lucifer's arms up to his elbows. Deep gashes cover his face, one across his cheek nearly down to the bone from where Abaddon clawed at him while he sawed through her wing.

Lucifer stands in her line of sight, the blood-soaked blade hanging loosely in his grip as if daring her to try again. Michael and, shockingly enough, Raphael stand on either side of him, each with a blade pointed at Abaddon.

Raphael is the first to swallow his horror and speak. "Abaddon, you have been found guilty of crimes against our Father's world and plotting to seize Heaven. You will serve as an example."

"Yes, she will." My voice sounds wrecked, whatever venom she poured down my throat ravaging my vocal cords more than years of screaming managed to. My steps are unsteady, but I manage to stay upright as I push away from Caila and walk to Raphael. I meet his eyes as I take the weapon from his hand.

I walk in front of Lucifer, blocking him from Abaddon's view. I do nothing until she looks up at me.

I smile at her, holding her gaze until the hatred in her eyes flickers into fear. I want her to ask for mercy. I want her to beg, but that has never been Abaddon's style.

I stab the blade into Abaddon's throat, and I watch until the light in her eyes finally goes out. Then I yank the blade from her body and hand it back to Raphael.

I make it a grand total of three steps before my knees give out and everything goes dark.

❧ 18 ❧

CAILA

They stare at me like I'm a ghost.

I land in the middle of a battle. Already exhausted and wrung out from my ordeal and the long flight home, I know any help I could offer would be useless.

All I see is Phenex stretched out on our front lawn, as still as death.

I hear the sick sound of flesh being hacked, and Abaddon screams a high, piercing wail of pain.

Our kind doesn't do well with true agony. We lack the frame of reference that humans have. When a bullet wound is no more distressing than a stubbed toe, our minds can't handle *true* pain.

I turn quickly enough to see the unmistakable look of horror across Raphael's face as he takes a step back from the blood-soaked scene. Ever the warrior, Michael looks unphased by the violence.

"You made this choice," Lucifer snarls as her severed wing comes away in his hands. He throws it into the street like refuse. "Let him go or I'll take the other one!"

I turn back to Phenex, staring down at his slack face and blank eyes, searching for any hint of movement. When her hold breaks on him, it's so abrupt that I nearly fall over with the shock.

Phenex stares at me like I'm something out of a dream before dragging himself to his feet to put an end to Abaddon on his own. I wonder whose face he's seeing when he looks down at Abaddon? Is it really hers, or is he staring at Brielle kneeling in the street?

It's not surprising when his body gives out the moment the adrenaline fades, leaving him slumped on the grass again.

I know how he feels.

The humans have a word for it. Closure.

I crouch beside Phenex, the stiff stems of the dried grass poking through the tears in my jeans. I brush my fingers over his brow, the lines of pain and fear finally erased by unconsciousness. His chest rises and falls slowly, free of whatever affliction Abaddon caused.

From my spot on the grass, I watch the archangels. I search the long years of my memories and try to remember the last time I saw those three standing together.

Lucifer looks numb, as though he can't quite believe what he just did, even if he doesn't regret doing it. Hell leaves scars, after all. I think Lucifer's realizing for the first time that he can leave Hell, but Hell won't ever fully leave him.

Wherever Grace is, I'm glad she wasn't here to witness this.

"What are you doing here?" I don't miss the accusation in Elissa's voice as she stares at Raphael. She trusts our little family of outsiders, but the archangel that told us we were on our own a day ago gets no quarter from her.

Raphael at least has the decency to look shamed by her words, but I can't bring myself to blame him. I know all too well how it feels to be under Heaven's thumb.

"I'm here on my own behalf, not Heaven's. I just couldn't walk away from what was happening here." He turns to address Michael and, after a brief hesitation, Lucifer. "Let me take her body to Heaven. I will *make* Metatron see that this goes beyond the petty squabbles of the past. This is not just one rogue demon slipping past the gates that Heaven can ignore."

Lucifer snorts. "You try that."

"I mean it, brother."

Lucifer tenses at the word. "Tread carefully, Raphael. Tread carefully. You may be willing to let the past lie, but I doubt Metatron has changed that much, even in a few thousand years."

Then Raphael is gone, those gleaming white wings taking him back to Heaven with Abaddon's body in tow like some grisly trophy.

Satisfied that Phenex is safe, I stand up, and suddenly three sets of eyes are on me, looking at me like they can't quite believe I'm real.

The dry grass crunches under my feet as I walk to where Michael and Lucifer are still standing in the middle of the empty street.

Lucifer looks me up and down, staring at me with scrutiny as if making certain that I really am Caila and not some copy that crawled out of Hell to torment them all further.

"You made it out then."

"I did."

There's so much more between those few words.

Abaddon's wing rests in the street between us like the carcass of some mighty bird, the blood gleaming like oil under the city lights.

I watch silently as Lucifer digs a lighter out of his suit pocket and flicks it open with a faint metallic clink. He stares down at the mass of black feathers for only a second before dropping the lighter. Even wet with blood the feathers catch quickly, and the flames light up his face.

"Lucifer." He doesn't look up at first, so I lean across the fire and press the snow white feather into his hand.

His hand shakes the slightest bit when he takes it. The plume glows brighter than the fire, brighter than the stars muted by the city lights.

"Where did you get this?" he demands, finally looking at me. There's desperation in his voice. There's sadness.

"You know where it came from."

Lucifer nods tightly before turning away and walking down the street alone.

"Roux sends his regards."

Elissa blanches at my words and nearly chokes on the glass of whiskey in her hand.

Phenex is tucked into my bed as he recovers, and I doubt an earthquake would rouse him right now.

But the three of us are far too wired to even consider the pretense of rest.

Michael stands by the front door, a silent watchman glaring out into the street. The wards are back up, but he can't bring himself to relax just yet.

Grace is holed up in her pretty house on the nice side of town. Her friend lived, and I suspect once the dust settles we'll have two more souls at our door, asking for answers.

Lucifer. . . Lucifer needs time. I wouldn't have presumed to say I knew him before this night, not really. I had vague memories of seeing him through the crowds in Heaven and centuries of listening to lies about his nature, that's all.

I know him now. I've seen where it all began. I've walked

that dark path and ripped through those thorns to finally reach the one place in Hell he wanted to hide.

The rest of us wear our scars on our skin. We've had that luxury. Lucifer has had to bury his for so long, he's convinced himself they don't exist.

Until tonight reminded him.

"Roux's in Hell?" Elissa's question pulls me out of my musings.

I nod. "If it's any consolation, he doesn't seem to mind it much."

Elissa sips her whiskey but doesn't ask for details. I suspect the morning will call for a more thorough explanation but for now, she lets it lie. Some part of Roux still exists, and he's not in torment.

For now, it's enough.

I perk up when I remember the flowers stuffed in my pockets. "I brought you a present!"

Elissa chuckles at my sudden enthusiasm. "Only you could find somewhere to shop in Hell." She leans forward with curiosity as I empty my pockets onto the table, careful not to miss a single precious petal. Her trepidation instantly changes into shocked joy as she realizes what the white flowers are.

"Is this asphodel?" When I nod, she's immediately up and rifling through the kitchen cabinets for a jar to collect every tiny piece.

"Thank you," she whispers once the final crumb of pollen has been secured. "This might save us one day, Caila. I mean it. This little jar is probably the most powerful thing in this house now." She places the jar down on the coffee table, staring at it like she's still amazed it exists. "You were in Hell and you stopped to pick flowers for me?"

I reach across the table and clench her fingers in mine. For so many decades it was just the two of us, fighting a losing battle to protect Serafine, Marianne, and finally Grace.

For so long it was us against the world, and with the sudden expansion of our circle, I think we both lost that.

"I'll always stop to pick flowers for you, even if you are a sarcastic witch who wears too much black."

Elissa laughs, instantly picking up the familiar game. "And you're a Heavenly princess that dresses like a cupcake."

Her smile falters the slightest bit at that, but she dares another comment. "For someone who hates my wardrobe so much, you sure steal a lot of it." When my own smile doesn't fade, Elissa ventures, "Does this mean you're going to start dressing like a debutant again?"

I think of the wardrobe stuffed with bright colors and soft fabrics, remnants of the Caila I used to be. I'd told myself it was foolish human vanity and that such things really shouldn't matter to me. That I shouldn't miss them. That I shouldn't miss being the person who wore them.

I think of that barren garden in Hell, every color leached from the plants, the trees, even the sky above, and I don't feel so foolish anymore.

PHENEX OPENS his eyes a few hours later.

The morning sun is streaming in through the cracks in the blinds, chasing away the darkness. The sounds of traffic filter in through the closed window as humans rush to work, to school, to wherever their lives might take them. Their tires roll over the fading scorch marks on the asphalt. A few more hours, and the last traces of Abaddon will be wiped clean.

The ruined clothing I wore through Hell is crumpled in a messy pile in the corner of the room. Even if the fabric wasn't pock-marked with tears and holes from the thorns, there's no amount of detergent that can erase the scent of Hell that permeates the fabric.

They smell like ashes. They smell like death. But I can't quite bring myself to throw them away yet. This time though, instead of raiding Elissa's closet, I open up mine.

I'm humming Sinatra as I flip through the clothes, staring at the colors bursting from the overfilled wardrobe. The pale blue dress I slip into isn't anything special. There are no distinct memories tied to that length of silk. I grab it nearly at random, pulling out the first thing I touch before I have a chance to change my mind.

The filmy fabric feels light against my body. It's not armor. It doesn't need to be.

The low rumble of Phenex's voice draws me back to the present in this small room. "I thought I died, but then I realized that couldn't be right because that would mean I was in Heaven."

To a human, those words would elicit a giggle. Just another cheesy line. But I know Phenex means every syllable. I crawl into the bed beside him, my quest to find a pair of shoes forgotten with the lure of the pale pink blankets and the one occupying them.

I pillow my head on his chest and listen to the familiar cadence of his heart.

Phenex's hands find my hair, and if I closed my eyes I could almost believe we were back there, alone in the darkness with nothing but each other to cling to.

I keep my eyes open.

"It's over. We made it."

We both know that's not true. The doors are sealed, but what escaped is still roaming free.

Asmodeus. Malphas. Astaroth. Azazel. They're still out there. And I'm not naïve enough to see Metatron as a potential ally, no matter what outcome Raphael might wish.

Phenex sits up and the cautiousness when he touches me is back. He doesn't know what I saw, after all. He doesn't know that I walked through Hell and came out stronger for it.

"I'm all right," I say, and I shock myself because I truly mean it. They aren't just words to reassure anyone else or a way to deflect a conversation I don't want to have.

A hot shower washed away the ash and blood. My wounds healed. My wings still ache from the thorns but even that's fading.

I saw the very start of Hell, and I clawed my way free.

I see the expectant look in Phenex's eyes. He wants to know the details. He wants to understand what I saw and what I felt down there. He spent millennia in Hell, but even after so much time, I suspect much of it is still a mystery to him.

He wants to share this with me, but I shake my head. The story isn't entirely mine to tell, not yet. I was crawling inside Lucifer's head, seeing his deepest, most painful secrets. I know what it means to be stripped bare like that, and I won't do it to him.

I brush my lips against Phenex, melting myself against him. I don't say anything else. I don't need to.

It isn't over. Outside there are still demons and Fallen roaming free. Raphael may forgive, but we are still Heaven's enemies.

But in this house, inside this small room, and wrapped in his arms the world finally feels right for the first time in too long.

❧ 19 ❧

PHENEX

I like the noise.

I wake up alone and buried in a tangle of pale pink cotton, and there's no frantic jolt back to awareness as I brace myself for the next attack. That animal part of my brain that demands constant vigilance can finally rest.

Sounds of life filter down the hallway through the half-open doorway, the creak of the kitchen cabinets and the clatter of dishes loud in the early morning.

This is different. This is new.

I pad down the hallway, my bare feet silent on the worn floors.

I hear Michael first. "How do you not own a spatula?"

Elissa cackles at his incredulous question. "Have we met?"

I follow the sound of her laughter to find Michael rifling through the barren refrigerator with a look of utter disdain on his face while Elissa and Caila giggle from the safe distance of the sofa.

Caila's arms are curled around one of the bright blue pillows, her cheeks flushed with laughter as she listens to Michael and Elissa's banter. After everything that's happened in the last days the entire scene is shockingly domestic and *human*.

I love it.

Soon enough, Grace and Lucifer will be at the door, and we'll all be drawn into more planning, more strategy.

Soon, but not yet.

For now, there is this, and it's *easy*. Michael crows with approval when he unearths a box of pancake mix from the recesses of one of the cabinets. He wipes away a thin coat of dust on the box that I'm begging to suspect came with the house. Elissa's laughing so hard at his reactions that she can barely catch her breath.

And Caila looks peaceful. Unafraid. For a moment I wonder if this is how she once was before Brielle tried so hard to snuff out her light, but I think better of it. The look she wears isn't the naïve smile of one who has never tasted bitterness or loss. She knows just how easy it would be for all of this joy to crumble to dust. She knows how precious every moment is, even for those of us that supposedly live forever.

I never thought this could be mine.

There is no loyalty in Hell. No friendships. No love. There are only favors and debts to be paid.

Lucifer alone was the exception.

I understand why the other Fallen lost themselves in the darkness.

I came close so many times, loneliness and isolation nearly driving me to become something I never wanted to be.

Elissa notices me hovering in the doorway, still so reluctant to disturb the happiness in front of me. "Phenex!" she exclaims, beckoning me into the room. "Michael has decided to attempt breakfast. Pray for all of us."

Home. For so long, I thought that place was Heaven, and I told myself that in my heart of hearts I regretted the choice I made all those years ago.

But you can't long for free will while still looking to lay the blame at another's feet.

I hated Hell as Lucifer did, hated the cruelty and the unrelenting ugliness of it all. I hated that we had both searched for freedom and instead ended up in a different set of shackles. In my weakest moments, I even hated myself for wanting to undo my choice, even if it meant sentencing my only friend to an eternity alone in the Pit.

For what? The memory of a gilded cage.

Elissa vacates her spot on the sofa, wandering into the kitchen with a cheerfully sarcastic, "Ingredients aren't going to magically appear out of thin air."

Without missing a beat, the archangel counters, "And you call yourself a witch."

I settle next to Caila, and she rests her head on my shoulder. I breathe in her scent, that heady mixture of lush flowers over the sharp scent of ozone. *Eden* my memory supplies, but in truth, I don't think I really remember what the air in the Garden smelled like anymore. But I can't imagine it being more perfect than this.

I curl my arm around her shoulders, smiling to myself when she nestles closer to me. It's hard not to wonder if all this is only because of what we endured together.

Maybe one day we still would have found our way to each other even if Brielle had never existed. Or maybe we would have stood forever on either side of the celestial aisle, never to meet in the middle.

Maybe if I had been a good little angel and ignored the Morningstar's words of freedom, I would have learned to be content with my lot in Heaven while Lucifer suffered in Hell alone.

Maybe if Caila had never slipped away from her post and deserted Uriel's cause, Grace would have never been born.

Michael would never have broken his own shackles, and Elissa would never have learned to forgive.

We've all lost too much time on maybes and might have beens.

Our love began in Hell, and I don't regret that. We sprang from the bleakest start possible, and we clawed our way toward the sun with the tenacity of a flower blossoming in the cracks of a city street.

After all, darkness always follows the light.

ACKNOWLEDGMENTS

To my readers - The fact that so many of you love this series as much as I do means the absolute world to me. Rest assured that I'm going to keep writing *Fire From Heaven* as long as you keep wanting to read it!

To Joe - I'm so glad you think all my crazy writer obsessiveness is cute. I love you.

To my Mom - The release of this book marks nearly ten years since I lost you. You always supported me, and I wish you could be here to share in this with me. I miss you.

Creating this universe and these characters is incredibly

rewarding, and hearing everyone's feedback has been wonderful!

Ava

ABOUT THE AUTHOR

Ava Martell was born on Friday the 13th, but she always believed in making her own luck and writing her own story. She is a firm believer that love really does conquer all, but sometimes you have to take the long way around to get there.

She lives in Austin, Texas with her husband, German Shepherd, and two deeply spoiled cats. Ava loves a good gin and tonic to wind her down or wind her up, depending on the occasion, and the only thing better than a good cocktail is a good story.

If you enjoyed this book, and want to receive information on any new books, sign up for Ava's mailing list here.

Follow Ava on social media

Facebook
Twitter
Tumblr
Instagram

Official site
avamartell.com

msavamartell@gmail.com

First Man

Throw out the rules.

Let the sparks fly.

And pray for a happily ever after. . .

Adam Edwards drifts in the wide world, searching for his next adventure. When his journey around the globe brings him to America he finds a love he never expects and a loss he can't endure.

Ember Pierson is 18 and counting down the days until graduation frees her from small town life. Everything changes when Adam rolls into town and takes a job teaching high school English, and Ember hatches a plan. . .

Printed in Great Britain
by Amazon